THE HOOD NOVELIST PRESENTS

Gangster Moves 1
The Homecoming

Yusuf Ali Mitchell

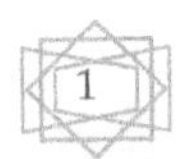

This is a work of fiction. The events and characters described herein are imaginary and not intended to refer to a specific place or living person. The opinions expressed in this manuscript are solely the opinions of the authors and do not represent the opinions or thoughts of the publisher.

The Hood Novelist
www.thehoodnovelist.com
ISBN- 9781513653747

DEDICATIONS

This book is dedicated to a few people that played a very major role in my life. My late father Isaac Mitchell Sr., my sister Yasheen Lewis, my right hand man John Niles (AKA Boo), Chantel Duncan of Seventh Street and the rest of my homies that I lost to the mean streets; Edmond (AKA Smooth), Boo Boo, Fat Mike, Richard Allen Asmar, Dor, Ant, Allen , Twin Horse, Love bug J.C. and anyone that I missed. Just know my fallen loved ones that you are missed each and everyday. Y'all are my motivation!

Special thanks to Shawn (Haqq) Sharp and Angela (Angel) Stevenson Ringo for their dedication. I almost forgot my main man Danny from the Seventh Street. You'll always be remembered. Seventh and Fifth Street stand up. Stop the violence out there. We all we got!

CHAPTER 1

The click clack of the dice in P-Love's hands was like music. He could feel the money in his pockets. All he needed was that number to hit one more time and he was out with enough paper to pay the rent while he got his shit together.

In the back of his mind he knew it was risky. Mickey was one of the biggest drug lords in South Carolina. The only thing was P-Love was a killer too. He'd done it all to survive in the streets. Loan sharking, hustling, slinging drugs, and gambling were just some of the skills in his repertoire.

He took a quick breath as he looked around the room one more time. He could see Mickey lookin down on him from the balcony. The man looked like murder incarnate, but that didn't matter to P-Love. Everybody was fair game if you was in the game, and it was time to take a chance before he drew the tip on himself.

He slung the dice with a prayer and the numbers came up. "Jackpot! Pay me motherfuckers!" He yelled as the dice danced across the felt table to hit his number.

The whole room was real quiet as P-Love counted his money out. A quiet that didn't seem to register right away to P-Love's ears in all of the excitement. Of course, two heavy hands on his shoulders got his attention real quick as he was spun to face Big Mickey and two of the club's bouncers.

"Damn Mickey man! What the fuck is all this shit about?"

"Snoop, let me see them dice that nigga just threw."

Snoop was an old drunk that Mickey had cleaned up and put to work because of his quick eyes. He watched everything, and was in everything. That's why niggahs got to calling him Snoop.

"I got em right here Mickey and they ain't the same one's that we started with. That's for damn sure!"

P-Love knew the jig was up. The sweat stains spreadin under his arms were a clear indication that he knew what Snoop was talkin about, and the consequences. What was Spooky as hell was that Mickey just kept right on wearing that wicked smile, but his hazel eyes weren't.

****

P-Love couldn't remember how he got into the ambulance. He kept hearing an angel telling him, "Hold on, everything was gonna be alright," like he was livin out an Al Green song, but the pain screamin out all over his body didn't seem to agree.

Last he could remember he was eatin lead pipes from head to toe and beggin for mercy. He faded in and out on the whole ride to Manning Hospital, and it took three days for him to fight his way out of a coma. In his dreams he kept hearing this beautiful angel talking to him, and at times he could feel someone holding his hand and telling him to just hang in there. In his mind, he clung to that hand as it shifted from the hand of who he thought his mother was, then shifted to his Grandmother who'd raised him.

That caring hadn't come often in P-Love's life so he cherished it and almost didn't want to come back to the cruel life he'd have to live surviving the way that he did.

Eventually, he fought his way back, and when he opened his eyes he thought he'd died and gone to heaven. It was hard to talk or look around with all the tubes in him. When he was finally able to find the strength to open his eyes he locked gazes on the sexy smile of the woman who'd saved him. A "DAMN!" would've been in order had he been in better condition, but since he couldn't talk, he just smiled and kept that shit to himself.

"I see you decided to join us again huh? I didn't think you was gonna make it after seein how I found you. I'm glad to see your gonna make it."

It was a wrap after that. Shirley had been his Florence Nightingale. She'd gone from watching the E.M.T. bring him into the emergency room where she worked the night shift, to falling in love with him. She'd seen everything there was to see of his lowest moment in life and he just had to make her his wife.

When P-Love was released from the hospital a few months later, he moved right into Shirley's house. It was a natural progression seeing as how Shirley's house was bought and paid for and he had no home of his own.

On July 20th, 1983, nine months after they moved in with each other, Shirley gave birth to twin baby boys. She named one Cam'ron and the other Cam'ren. P-Love looked down on his children with tears in his eyes as he brushed his hands through his wavy hair with a few wisps of grey starting to show.

"I'm so proud of you baby! You brought us two healthy baby boys into this world!" He said as he took each of his newborn sons into his arms for the first time.

"No. We did it!" Shirley said while looking up at her man proudly.

To see her face and the beautiful child that she'd given him meant everything to P-Love. It was settled in his mind. Shirley was the love of his life and she deserved his commitment.

"Baby will you marry me?" He asked after putting their sons down into the two little cribs the nurses had put into Shirley's room.

He turned around and looked at a stunned Shirley. Then he walked over to her bedside and got down on one knee while going into his pocket to retrieve a black box that held a five carat diamond ring. He held it out to Shirley as he opened it and asked her again. "Baby will you marry me?"

Shirley just sat there speechless and in shock. "Is that a yes or a no baby? You know I love you."

With tears in her eyes, Shirley said, "Yes I'll marry you."

Shirley had never met a man like P-Love, and definitely not one who gave her the love that she knew she deserved. It wasn't that she wasn't beautiful that made men dog her. It was just the opposite. She'd been dogged out "because" of it and found that if dudes didn't outright take advantage of her because of how kind hearted she was, they were just too scared to approach her because of how attractive she was.

Shirley was eye candy to say the least. She was a mixture of Black and Indian, and it showed in her high cheek bones, fat round ass, and long straight black hair that hung down to her back. She was red bone thick in all the right places, and now she would be P-Love's woman for life.

P-Love proudly put the ring on Shirley's finger and kissed her gently on the lips. He could see that giving birth had taken a lot out of her, and although he didn't want to let her go right at that moment he had to be unselfish and let her sleep after the ordeal of giving birth to his two sons.

Two weeks after Shirley was released from the hospital Shirley and P-Love stood side by side in her backyard getting married. It was the best day of Shirley's life since she'd finally married the man of her dreams. As she turned after they'd both said their I do's, she looked out to each of the guests that had attended the wedding. All of her co-workers were there from her job. Her girlfriend Lisa was her maid of honor and the first to congratulate her.

Everyone was happy and in all the excitement of the ceremony, Shirley never noticed that many of her female co-workers were sliding seductive looks at her new husband. Especially, her best friend Lisa.

***** Three Years Later *****

Shirley was happy and settled into married life with P-Love. She'd gotten him a janitorial job working at the hospital and in the beginning of their marriage things were just fine with her. They appeared to have the perfect Cosby marriage.

Eventually P-Love became bored with the straight life. He was a hustler by nature and those streets just kept calling him.

At first the fear of Mickey knowing that he'd actually survived his beat down had been enough to keep him in check and out of the city. But as time progressed, he slid back into his old ways and started hooking up with some of his old homies in the city.

Shirley started to see a pattern of P-Love coming home later and later each night. She had hoped that his late night forays would eventually subside and that it was just something he had to get out of his system.

She feared for him constantly. P-Love never told her much about why someone had tried to kill him and she didn't ask too many questions for fear that she would push him away.

That changed when she started finding women's numbers inside of his pockets. It wasn't that she was snooping or insecure. She had to wash his clothes and didn't want to wash his money. She'd never expected that he would cheat on her, but she knew that one and one equaled two. Staying out late and having women's numbers in your pockets meant you were doing something.

When the phone started ringing at all hours of the night with people hanging up on you, she knew that P-Love was up to no good, so she started paying even more attention to what was going on around her.

She started to notice how Lisa and P-Love were always so cordial with each other. At first she thought it was just because Lisa was her best friend and because they worked together.

Now she knew better and suspected that even if it wasn't Lisa, it was other women, and she suspected everybody.

At night she would lay patiently tracking what time P-Love came home. She listened to his excuses and often times cried herself to sleep. The stress of worrying about their relationship seemed to be taking a toll on her body too. She began to lose weight and watch as her hair grew thinner. Her hair lost its beautiful luster and her skin took on a sickly tinge.

Shirley suspected that it was from all of the stress that she was dealing with as well as all of the hours that she'd worked. That along with keeping up with the kids was wearing her out physically and emotionally.

One night she just sat up in her bed waiting for P-Love to come home. Her wall clock read 4:00 a.m. and P-Love still hadn't come home.

She was getting tired of his shit, and although he'd come home late before, P—Love had never come home this late.

The late nights coming home smelling like sex had taken their toll, in her mind she knew that shit had to stop. She knew that the sex smell wasn't from her since P-Love hadn't made love to her in next months. She made up her mind to put a stop to the dumb shit once and for all.

She had everything cut off in the house and just waited for P-Love. She wanted to hear exactly when his cheating in ass came prancing through the door.

When she heard the front door open and close, she laid down in the bed and played sleep. Moments later, their bedroom door crept open. P-Love slid in trying to make as little noise as possible so he wouldn't wake her.

Little did he know that Shirley was already awake and waiting on his no good ass.

He took off his snake skin shoes and put them near the door. He then tip toed over towards their bed to see if Shirley had heard him. Just as he leaned over, Shirley popped up on the bed scaring the hell out of P-Love.

"I know you ain't tryna creep yo' funky ass into this bed!" She yelled.

P-Love nearly shit his pants as he jumped back scared out of his mind.

"Woman, what the hell is wrong with you scarin me like that?!? I coulda had a heart attack you crazy bitch!"

In the next room the twins woke up from all the screaming and commotion. They'd never heard their parents argue and it scared them to death. They both grabbed each other and cautiously walked down the hall to their parent's bedroom door. P-Love and Shirley continued to argue not realizing that they'd awakened their children.

"What the hell are you talkin about woman? I was workin late!"

P-Love wasn't lying about that since he'd just ripped one of the city's crap houses a new ass hole by winning $15,000. The only part he left out was that he'd treated himself to a shot of some good pussy from her girlfriend Lisa in celebration of having gotten one of Mickey's clubs for so much money.

As they argued, Shirley looked over and saw her twins standing in the doorway. They looked ready to defend their mother P-Love lowered his voice too as he got right up in her face so the kids wouldn't hear them arguing.

"Look I don't have time for this shit tonight I do everything I need to do to make sure you and our boys have a roof over your heads. I ain't goin for all this bitchin tonight!" He said trying to put his foot down.

Little did he know that Shirley had something for his ass. "Oh yo' ass is going to have time for it or I'm taking the twins and leavin yo' no good ass!"

P-Love was shocked. He got right up in her face with venom in his voice.

"Over my dead body! You'll never take my boys from me!" That's when he stepped back and started taking off his clothes.

Shirley just looked at him as if he had lost his mind if he thought he was gonna jump on her good clean sheets without washing the pussy funk from another woman off first.

"You ain't jumpin your pussy smellin ass up in this bed. You can sleep on the couch tonight!" She said as she jumped off their bed in one swift motion and pushed him out of the way. She stepped to their bedroom door and gave him one last evil look as she went to go check on the twins.

P-Love just looked at her and walked towards his dresser where he grabbed a fresh pair of underwear. He walked out of their room with some fresh underclothes heading for their bathroom. While he was in the shower, Shirley came back into the room and went through his pockets looking for any girls numbers. She didn't find anything incriminating and for that she was grateful. She looked at the money he'd thrown on the bed and just shook her head. She was grateful for the money, but she knew that was cheating in too. She hoped that she'd gotten her point across.

She loved P-love to death and would gladly give her life for him and her children if need be. She just wanted the same respect, and love in return.

In the next room Cam'ran and Cam'ron lay quietly wondering what their parents were arguing about. They were afraid and they could see that something was wrong with Mommy and Daddy.

CHAPTER 2

It was December of 1985 and only a few days before Christmas. The boys were anticipating the coming holiday. Throughout the weeks leading up to Christmas Shirley hadn't been feeling very well. She'd set up an appointment with her Doctor for later on that day when she got to work. She should've said something sooner since she'd been getting constant migraines and couldn't figure out why. That coupled with her lack of appetite was something that she suspected was probably from stress.

She tried to get up and get the kids ready to go. Her stomach kept turning as she made her way to the kitchen. In an instant her head was spinning and she blacked out while reaching for a frying pan under the kitchen sink.

BLAM! CLANK-LANK-LANK!

P-Love jumped out of the bed wondering what the hell all of the noise was so early in the morning. He called to Shirley and got no answer.

That worried him since she never let him keep calling her when the kids were sleep. He got up and went down the hall to the kitchen and when he turned the corner he saw his wife passed out.

P-Love was so frightened that he didn't even

hear his children come sleepwalking up behind him as he tried to wake Shirley up.

"Shirley baby! Get up! What's wrong with you! Please baby wake up!

It wasn't until the kids started crying behind him that he knew they were there. Panicked he grabbed the kitchen phone off the wall and dialed 911. He had to yell over Cam'ron and Cam'ren as they hugged their mother and begged her to wake up.

He gave the operator the information as calmly as he could and stayed on the phone as he cradled his wife's head in his lap while trying to calm the boys down.

When the E.M.T. arrived, Shirley was taken to Manning Hospital where both of them had worked for years. Shirley received the best care that they could give and was finally revived. When she woke up, P-Love was right there holding her hand to comfort her.

Shirley's first thought was that she might have just been pregnant or something. All P-Love knew was that the doctors didn't say exactly what was wrong with Shirley, but were running tests.

All her girlfriends were coming in and out of the room checking on her and caring for the twins. Lisa's sneaky ass was there too to lend her own moral support.

Shirley looked over to P-Love when she was finally able to speak.

"What happened?"

"I don't know baby. I found you passed out in the kitchen. Let me go tell Dr. Sharpe that you're awake."

He let go of her hand and rushed out to get the doctor for her. He was so relieved to see that his wife was awake that he couldn't see the jealous look in Lisa's eyes as she watched over his kids.

Moments later, the Doctor came in following P-Love. "How are you feeling Shirley?" Asked Dr. Sharpe.

"I feel so weak!" She said while looking back at the doctor.

Dr. Sharpe retrieved the clip board from the foot of her bed and began to review her records. His face turned very troubled as he stepped away and started checking the test results more intently. When he was done, he looked up with a saddened expression written on his face.

"Dr. Sharpe, what is it? What's wrong with me?"

Dr. Sharpe got up out of the chair and came back to hold Shirley's hand as he spoke. "Shirley, I'm sorry to be the one to have to tell you this but you have cancer."

P-Love damn near fell as his knees buckled. He had to hold onto the railing of the bed just to stand back up as tears began to slowly drift down the sides of Shirley's cheeks.

When P-Love was able to regain his composure, he asked the doctor, "Isn't there something we can do Doc?"

Dr. Sharpe shook his head. "We'll wait for the other tests to come back for a more conclusive answer, but I can tell you that it doesn't look good. I've known you both a long time and I wish there was more that we could do. Had we caught this sooner we might have been able to control it. But from all the tests in your chart it looks like the cancer has spread throughout your lymphatic system. If I'm right-- and I pray to God I'm not -- you have a number of tumors that have metastasized. If that's the case, then there's nothing we can do."

Shirley knew what he was saying. She was dying and there was nothing that could be done for her. She looked at P-Love and saw the hatred he had in his eyes for the doctor. He was a fighter his whole life and just couldn't give up. He just couldn't accept life without his wife.

"So what the fuck are you saying Doc!"

The doctor stayed calm. He understood the bitterness that P-Love was feeling.

"There's nothing we can do at this point. The cancer has run its course through her entire body. At this point I don't think chemo can help. If we would've found it a month or maybe even a year earlier, in its beginning stages, we could have done something for her."

Shirley could see P-love's confusion so she tried to interrupt. "Baby, it's going to be alright."

"No it's not. What about our boys? What about us? I can't live without you."

Shirley cried then as the weight of death

came crashing into her reality. She'd found her love and given birth to two sons. She'd finally seen some semblance of happiness. The only thing that kept her going was trying to keep P-Love together for the children.

"I'm dying, but you have to take care of the twins. You have to be strong for them."

P-Love wasn't having it. "Don't worry baby. You and our boys are going to be okay. I'm going to call around and see who can help you. We'll get a second opinion from another doctor."

The doctor was resolute. "Sir, we're the best doctors in the state at treating cancer. You and Mrs. Monday have worked in this building, so you know that we can provide the best care available."

Shirley knew this better than anyone. From her experience she knew it was the truth. She'd ignored the symptoms she'd seen so many of her patients suffering from, she tried to end the conversation.

"Doctor I know your telling me the truth. We've been friends for years, and I appreciate everything that you've done for us. Can you just give me the medication and send me home?"

The doctor appreciated her kind words. He squeezed her hand gently. "Look, we'll keep you here for a few more weeks to give you the medication before sending you home with it."

P-Love interrupted, "So you just going to send my wife home to die?"

He looked at the doctor like it was all his

fault.

"Mr. Monday, that's all we can do at this point."

"What about chemotherapy?" P-Love asked bitterly.

The doctor looked at Shirley before responding. She looked hopeful, so he relented.

"If that's what Shirley wants, then we can give it a try. I just think it's too late."

****

Two weeks later after Shirley had started taking chemotherapy, she started showing signs of improvement. The symptoms that she experienced from the medication made her insides feel raw and she stayed in pain constantly. Eventually it became too much for her, especially after the tests came back confirming that she wasn't going to make it.

She decided that the benefits would only be temporary and opted not to take anymore of the chemo. She told the doctors that she didn't want it anymore and wanted to be released, so that she could spend the last few days she had left at home with her family.

When she came home she was bed ridden. She stayed in her room waiting to die while P-Love went between caring for her and the kids as best as he could. She could see the changes in him as she withered away. It was like torture to see his wife slowly dying.

The twins were five years old. They saw that their mother didn't look anything like her once beautiful self. Her hair had fallen out and her once voluptuous body had shriveled to a cruel husk of what it once had been.

The twins became frightened of her. It wasn't that they thought she was ugly. They truly loved their mother. It was just that they felt helpless to do anything for her and began to take their frustrations out on each other. They began to bicker and fight over everything since they didn't know how to deal with the anger they felt at slowly losing their mother.

It got so bad that she finally asked Lisa to take them to her house to be looked after. Lisa still brought them by to see their mother each and every day. The guilt of what she'd done behind Shirley's back with her husband served to eat at her too as she gained weight.

The jealousy of P-Love not having eyes for anyone, but Shirley tore at her too, but she tried to hold it together for all of them.

P-Love took to drinking heavily. He was off his gambling game and would leave the house for days at a time. He refused to let go of his wife and couldn't take seeing her in the state that she was in.

He was grateful that the hospital did everything that they could to make sure that she was comfortable. The nurses that she'd worked with for years all took turns caring for her when he wasn't there. Especially since P-Love began to take his frustration out on everyone around him.

Many times he prayed. He promised God that if he would save his wife he would praise him every Sunday. The sad part is, God had other plans....

*****One Month Later*****

"Brothers and Sisters, we are gathered here today to say our final farewells to Sister Shirley Monday. A beloved friend, a loving wife, and child that God has called back unto himself, she was a good spirit from God that gave light to everyone that she came in contact with. If you needed anything, Sister Shirley was there lend a helping hand!"

Amens could be heard as the congregation of women flagged themselves with fans scrolled with advertisements and church figures.

P-Love, Cam'ren, and Cam'ron sat in the first row as the minister extolled the virtues of their mother and wife. Lisa was there with them, sobbing uncontrollably as she listened intently to the sermon.

The minister spoke for 15 minutes about the virtuous person that Shirley had been. When he was done. He called on P-Love to come and give his final words as her husband. P-Love was lost. Something inside of him had snapped and he couldn't move. Lisa tried to get his attention and it was like he ignored everything around him except for the woman that laid before him in the casket.

The preacher, seeing that P-Love was unable to speak, continued his sermon as the women in the pews clucked and sucked their teeth like old hens. Many of the women in the pews were women who knew that P-Love was a cheater since they were the ones cheating with him.

The twins watched all of this with tear stained cheeks as the somber funeral concluded.

Their mother was gone and the only thing they had left was a broken hearted father to cling to.

CHAPTER 3

(Eight Years Later)

The twins had just turned thirteen years old. They'd watched as their father began to change over the years. He didn't spend a lot of time at home anymore. He'd taken to constantly staying drunk and bringing all types of women home. They were pretty much left to fend for themselves after everyone who'd been in their mother's life started to come by less and less after her death.

They still constantly fought, but they also took out a lot on the kids that they went to school with. Cam'ron started cutting school early rather than keep getting his ass whipped by his father for getting into fights.

Cam'ren did good at school when his brother wasn't around. It was like Cam'ron was his evil twin and he was his brother's good half. Together they kind of balanced each other out, but when Cam'ron was alone, he got into all types of trouble.

They had in his mind that he wanted to be a gangster like his father. He'd been caught numerous times playing with his father's guns and no matter what his father did it was like he was obsessed with them.

Cam'ren didn't care for it. It was just that he loved his brother. He was all he had and if his brother got into anything, he was always right there with him. Even if he didn't like the people his brother hung out with, he stuck it out because of love for his brother.

At night, they would wait for their father to come home. Cam'ron got the idea to wait and see if his father got dressed up to date one of his lady friends. His father would often bring home beautiful women and it excited him to listen to his father wear those old bitches out.

When he saw that his father was talking to one of his female friends on the phone before going out, he knew it was on that night. He convinced Cam'ren to hide with him in their father's closet, but before they did they drilled little holes in the door so they could watch what their father did to the woman they knew he would bring home that night.

As they hid waiting for him to come in, they both fell asleep. They were jolted awake as they heard their father stumbling into his room in a drunken stupor.

The woman had big tits squashed in a tight yellow dress with deep chocolate skin. The shit looked horrible against her dark skin, but her body was crazy!

They listened as their father just kept talking, "Maaan fuck that bitch Mickey! I done broke his ass again and he ain't gonna do shit about it!"

The chick just laughed with him and then started rubbing the front of their father's pants.

Cam'ron got real excited and kept elbowing Cam'ren. Cam'ren could see what was going on and didn't really get what all the fuss was about, so he just watched.

"Baby you was hot tonight! You done got me even hotter. Let me get some this good sausage you got swangin in dem slacks!"

P-Love laughed. "You damn right I'm hot and I'ma wear dat ass out too!" He dug in his pockets and pulled out a big wad of money along with a pair of dice. He pushed the chocolate chick down on the bed and then threw the money and dice all over her body in a drunken attempt to make it rain.

The dice hit the chick in the forehead and she grabbed them tryna figure out what the hell he hit her in the head with.

"Maaan, what the hell you hittin me in the head wit?"

Then she looked closer so she could see that they looked alot like the dice that Mickey used at his club.

She showed them to P-Love and said, "What you do, take da damn dice from the game?"

P-Love grabbed the dice and hurried up trying to hide the dice. He knew she wasn't supposed to see that he had them since, if Mickey found out he was makin the switch, he knew Mickey would kill him this time for sure.

"Shhhhh! I got somethin for you baby," he

said as he started rubbing up inside her thick chocolate legs. The chick moaned and started gyratin her hips like crazy, as her ass cheeks started pokin out the side of her dress.

P-Love kissed her real deep as he slid the thin spaghetti straps of her dress off of her shoulders and then exposed one ample breast.

He started squeezin the titty real good as he worked his way down the side of her neck.

The Dark skinned chick moaned, Oooh Daddy! Das my spot!"

P-Love lingered a little while just teasin her on the neck as he fingered her wet and milky insides real good. Then he slid down a little lower and took her one exposed breast into his mouth and licked it like he was slurpin on a pacifier.

The woman started coming all over his hands and that got both the boys' attention. They had never seen what their father had done to the women he brought home. Now they were getting to see firsthand what all the fuss was about and they both liked it.

Cam'ren looked over at his brother and saw the boy was droolin all ever himself. He could feel his little pencil dick pushin against his Pee-Jays as he watched his brother just holdin himself down there like he was in pain or somethin.

He turned back just in time to see the hairy bush peekin out under the woman's dress. Her clit looked all big and swollen like his own private parts, and he was amazed since he never knew a woman's insides looked like that.

His father kicked off his gator boots and started undoin his pants as he kissed the woman. When his pants dropped down to his ankles, his dick popped up like a striking black mamba and damn near hit the woman dead across the lips.

Her eyes got real big as she looked at the full length of P-Love. P-Love looked down with pride at the surprise written all over the woman's face.

"Now you gon find out why they call me P-Love," he said as he slid his dick across the bright red lip stick stained lips of the chocolate sister he had in front of him.

It took her both hands just for her to guide his massive dick into her waiting mouth.

She gulped and slid the dick as far as it would go down her throat then slurped, as it popped back out of her red juicy lips. She spit on the dick to lube it up then smacked her lips down on it again in the blink of an eye all the way to the base of his 10½ inch shaft without gaggin one bit!

P-Love grabbed her by her tight curls and started makin love to her face with slow deep thrusts.

The boys could see every muscle in their father's ass cheeks as he tightened and released in a slow grind that seemed to delight the dark skinned woman to no end.

Suddenly P-Love began to moan, as he shot load after load of hot white liquid all over the woman's face. The boys could see it cause the woman was so black!

When he was done shootin his load, the woman wiped her face and removed the lip-stick she had on with a dirty towel P-Love had beside his bed.

He stood workin himself up and down his shaft to stay hard as he waited for her to get cleaned up. When she was done, he stood her up, smacked her on her big chocolate ass, hiked up her neon yellow miniskirt, and started slidin up in her from the back.

Inch by inch he disappeared between her chocolate cheeks as she moaned in delight.

"Das right! I want all dat dick Daddy. Give it to me!"

P-Love started plowin into the woman. Each time he slid all the way to the hilt, he would quick pound the ass with rapid thrusts real deep inside of her and then slide out as he smacked her on her ass cheeks to make her fuck him harder.

Before long, P-Love and the woman were moaning in delight as they got down to a rhythm.

Slap, slap, slap, slap, slap real fast then Pop! He would smack that ass.

The woman's knees damn near buckled as she started coming.

"Awe shit Daaaaaady I'm gonna cooooooooome." She cooed as P-Love stroked her even faster. The boys watched as cum ran down the woman's legs like spilled cream across a burnt skillet. In minutes her pussy started making weird squish sounds like she was farting over and over again.

The boys had to control themselves from laughing at the weird noises the lady's coochie was makin.

Their father started moanin real hard and soon he was shakin with every stroke. "Move dat ass girl! Give it to me now. Daddy bout ta blow a load!"

The boys could see their father break stride as he shook with his dick deep inside the woman's chocolate cheeks. Slowly he slid out when he was done and started crawlin across the bed. Within minutes he was fast asleep as the woman sat smokin a cigarette.

She looked over at P-Love then picked up one of the dice that had fallen out of his pocket back onto the bed. She held it up to the night light, then tucked it in her purse and turned off the light.

When they boys heard the woman snoring like a pig in heat they snuck cut of the closet and made their way to their room. They both were excited as hell.

"See I told you we was gonna have some fun tonight. Daddy done wore that bitch out!" Cam'ron said as he crawled up on the top bunk above his brother and then peeked over.

Cam'ren didn't say much. It felt like he had to pee real bad and he felt wet inside his underwear.

"We gotta do that shit again man! You

gonna watch with me tomorrow night?"

Cam'ren agreed, then rolled over and went to sleep holding himself as his brother quietly beat his dick for the first time above him like he'd seen his father doing.

****

They didn't hear when the dark-skinned woman left their house. Their father came and woke them up late so they could go to school.

Both of them couldn't wait to see what would happen the next time their father brought a woman home. They hurried straight home after school to wait for their father.

P-Love came in late from work that night and they didn't think that he would be going out that night. Around 7 o'clock the phone rang and it was Rina, the chick that P-Love had sexed the night before. Cam'ren went and handed his father the phone in the living room before going back into the kitchen to finish his dinner.

"Who was it man?" Cam'ron asked in a whisper when his brother sat back down at the table.

"I think it was dat lady from last night."

Cam'ron started smiling with a wicked grin and tryna listen to what his father said on the home. In a minute his father came back into the kitchen and hung up the phone.

"Y'all make sure y'all do your homework and then take yo asses straight to bed. I gotta go out tonight. Aiight?"

"Yes sir," they both answered as their father went into his room.

As soon as they heard his door shut so he could get ready, Cam'ron was all up on Cam'ren about watching what would happen again that night.

Of course Cam'ren wanted to see too, so they waited for their father to leave, then went straight to the closet where they fell asleep again. When they woke up it was pretty late and they were both kind of hungry.

"Yo, we need some snacks for the show tonight," said Cam'ron.

Cam'ron took the hint. "Let me run real quick and grab something for us to eat."

He shot out of the closet and ran into the kitchen. He grabbed two bowls out of the cabinet and filled them each with cheese puffs and popcorn like they used to eat when they went to the movies. He took one look out the window to make sure his father wasn't coming, then ran back into the room to the closet and closed the door.

Neither of them even cared if they had to eat while smelling funky socks and dirty underwear their father had thrown into the closet. They just sat and waited patiently until their father came home.

After about another 45 minutes they heard the front door open and bang against the foyer wall. They could hear the muffled giggles of more than one person and rose up on their knees toget a good look when their father and his friend came in.

They got more and more excited as they listened to the shuffle of their father's footsteps in expectation of another peep show, and weren't disappointed when their father brought two new women into the room with him.

Both of the women were tall and thick red bones like their father usually liked his women. To Cam'ron and Cam'ren they were the prettiest women that they'd ever seen.

The three embraced and began kissing each other making a sandwich out of their father as one woman stood in the front while the other stood in back.

They could tell that P-Love was good and drunk as he fought to keep his balance between the two women while they felt him and each other up.

The women wasted no time getting right down to business. They worked like a tag team unit pulling P-Love out of his clothes piece by piece as they kissed and licked each inch of flesh that they exposed.

P-Love just laid back like a pampered baby enjoying all the attention that the two women paid to his body.

To Cam'ren and Cam'ron's disbelief, the woman in front pulled down their father's pants and started sucking his dick then his balls while the other one started licking his ass hole.

P-Love just moaned and squirmed in delight as the woman behind him worked her tongue along the crack of his ass tossin his salad like a chef.

Within minutes the two women had P-Love undressed and splayed across the bed, as one woman sat on his face, while the other one rode his face like it was a bicycle seat. P -Love worked his tongue along the slit of her pussy then rapidly flicked his tongue in a teasing motion over her clit. The woman squirmed and panted in ecstasy as she gyrated her hips in a back and forth motion over P-Love's mouth.

The other woman braced herself on P-Love's chest as she squatted down along the length of P-Love's thick manhood. When he felt her slide down his hands rose up to grab her by the hips and guide her down the full length of his love stick.

The red bitch pulled up and tried to resist takin it all in, but P-Love began to thrust his hips upward to force her to take it all as he pushed down with his hands on her hips.

Her eyes rolled back in her head as the boys watched the meat between their father's legs get slick with the juices of the woman riding him.

It wasn't long before all three of them found their rhythm as P-Love deep stroked upward into the squatting woman's guts. The boys watched the woman's fat ass as their father slid in and out in deep strokes while she rode him.

In all the excitement the boys didn't see the

woman riding their father's face reach into her ample bra and pull out a straight razor, she moaned as she came with her friend who started riding P-Love even faster, and as they both came together, the woman on P-Love's face drew back and slit his exposed throat.

Their father spasmed like a dying fish as he tried to speak. The two women stood up over him on top of the bed, then the one that was riding his face bent over and looked him dead in his eyes, and said, "You shouldn't bring crooked dice to other people's establishment. Mickey let you live once you dumb motherfucker. You shoulda left well enough alone."

With that, she wiped the bloodied blade off on his sheets, put the razor away, and turned to her friend. "Aloe check dat niggah pockets. We might as well take the money, so it looks like a robbery." With that, the chick ridin the dick stepped down and took the money their father had won that evening while the other one took his jewelry.

The boys just sat stunned and in shock at what they had just witnessed. They were both too afraid to do anything for fear that the women would kill them next, so they hid under all the stinking laundry and prayed the women wouldn't look in the closet.

The women didn't open the closet door, and when they heard footsteps leading to the front door, they both found the courage to peek.

Their father's bloodied body lay limply

across the bed. The smell of sex mixed with the sickly sweet smell of blood and shit hit their noses since their father's bowels had evacuated.

They jumped when they heard the door slam and waited for nearly a half an hour before they dared come out. Cam'ron crawled over to his father's soiled body and looked into his glossy eyes.

"Daddy! Daddy please don't be dead. We need you Daddy! Who else is gonna take care of us?" His cries went unanswered.

His father died within minutes from blood loss and a loss of oxygen.

Cam'ren ran out of the room and went straight to the phone in the kitchen after locking the front door.

"911 What is your emergency?" The woman on the other end of the line inquired through her nasal voice.

"Somebody killed my Daddy! He ain't breathin and we need help!"

"Is the person who did this to your father still in the house young man?" Cam'ren looked out the front room window hoping and praying the two women were long gone.

"No Ma'am. I think they gone, but my daddy is cut up real bad!"

"Well what is your address young man so we can send someone right over?"

Cam'ren conveyed their home address and stayed on the line until the police arrived. In all that time his brother never came out of the room and Cam'ren was too afraid to go back there. It made him think too much of seeing his dead mother.

When the police arrived they nearly broke the door down as they made their way by force into the house with guns drawn. This scared Cam'ren more than anything as he peed his pants thinking the two women had come back to kill him.

The police cuffed him like he was the criminal.

They searched the house asking him, a lot of questions that he couldn't answered since he was so afraid. In all the commotion it never dawned on him that his brother hadn't been seen.

Eventually, a fat boss hog looking white man with a pound of fat hanging off the back of his neck and chewing tobacco walked into the living room to take charge. He introduced himself to Cam'ren as Sheriff Brown, and instructed one of his men to unhandcuff him as he spoke to him. The E.M.T. unit arrived and began loading their father onto the gurney. Cam'ren could see them put the sheet over their father's face from the living room as he hung his head.

As the E.M.T. unit moved by with the body, one of the men told Sheriff Brown that P-Love was dead.

"Is anyone else in of the house young man?" Sheriff Brown asked as they wrapped up the crime scene.

"No sir! Everything is clear." Stated one of the officers.

Sheriff Brown turned and looked down on Cam'ren. "Boy do you have any relative you can stay with until we sort this mess out."

Cam'ren couldn't think of anyone he could call for help, so he answered, "No."

"Well, you'll have to come down to the station with us until we can get social services to pick you up and give you a place to stay."

Tears came down Cam'ren's face leaving fresh streaks as proof of all he had endured that night. He looked up at the sheriff and asked, "Why do I have to go to jail?"

The officer spit in his little Styrofoam cup while looking at Cam'ren sideways, then answered, "Cuz you ain't got no family, boy! I can't just leave you here in this house. Whose gonna look after you?"

He could tell that Sheriff Brown felt sorry for him. There just wasn't anything that he could do and Cam'ren still didn't know where his brother had gone to. Cam'ren accepted his fate as he got up and left the only home he'd ever known.

****

Cam'ron laid hidden in the attic above the body of his dead father. He'd climbed up through the crawl space by the ladder that led into the hall and pulled the ladder back up into the crawl space. He put the plywood cover back over the trap door and waited for everyone to leave. He knew his brother wouldn't tell on him. Their father had always told them to climb up there and hide if anybody ever came to the house to try to hurt their family.

Plus, Cam'ron knew that their father hid all his guns up in the crawl space along with most of the money he'd won. Cam'ron waited until he heard the front door close, then watched as the ambulance and police cars took his father and brother away. Then, he crawled over his father's duffel bag and looked for his gun. He found the money his father had hiding along with a small composition book that had names and addresses of all the people who owed him money.

He flipped through the pages as his young mind plotted revenge. He just had to figure out who Mickey was and why he'd had his father killed. He also had to find out where his brother was.

He also remembered that one of the women's names was Aloe. She'd held his father down while the other woman cut his father's throat.

He vowed then and there to kill everyone who destroyed his family. A vow he would die to make come true....

CHAPTER 4

Cam'ron went to the first name that he saw in his father's book the next morning. He jumped on his mountain bike and headed over to Mr. Jerry's house.

Mr. Jerry was a big time drug dealer who had his ups and downs messing with heroin, going to crap houses where he lost a lot of his money, and kept getting himself into debt all the time. That's how P-Love and him started dealing with each other. P-Love was a notorious loan shark, gambler, and occasional drug dealer.

Cam'ron jumped off his bike after riding the distance from his house to Mr. Jerry's. He put down the kickstand and adjusted his Eddie Bauer jacket to better conceal his father's 38 Special.

Mr. Jerry opened the door and looked down on Cam'ron with his massive 6'4", 300 pound frame filling up the foyer hallway.

"What's up young buck?" Mr. Jerry asked with a smile while scratching himself through piss and food stained boxer shorts that looked like he never washed them.

Cam'ron hunched up his shoulders gathering courage from the cooling reassurance of the gun in his coat and said, "I would like to come in and talk to you if you don't mind."

"About what?" Mr. Jerry asked as he looked down at the little sweaty kid.

Cam'ron looked around like he thought someone might overhear his conversation and it made Mr. Jerry look around too like someone might be watching him.

"You in some kind of trouble boy? I heard what happened to your father. Is that what this is about?"

Cam'ron just nodded and gripped a little tighter on the 38.

"Which one are you anyway? I can't never tell neither one of you boys apart."

"I'm Cam'ron", Cam'ron said as he looked back over his shoulder again.

Mr. Jerry scratched himself then stepped to the side to let the boy in. Cam'ron scrunched up his nose, tried to hold his breath when he brushed up against the rolls of fat that hung off the man, and slid past stepping into the living room.

The place was filthy. There were pizza boxes, beer cans, fast food rappers from burgers, and all types of other shit strewn all across the room.

One purple chair in a corner had the cushions so sunk in from Jerry's fat ass sitting in it that it looked more like a plaster print of his butt crack than a cushion.

An old T.V. with aluminum foil sat rolling up and down every few seconds with the vertical hold fucked up, and the whole place smelled like dirty socks someone kept playing ball in without washing them until their feet turned sour.

Cam'ron moved to what looked like a couch and cleared some of the trash so he could sit down while Jerry took his throne on the old purple chair.

"So what's up young buck?"

Cam'ron wanted to cry just thinking about the last time his father had brought him here. He controlled himself and let his anger give him courage for what had to be done.

"I came here to get the money you owed my Daddy."

Jerry's eyes went up in surprise.

"What? Yo' father is dead! So the money I owe him is dead too!"

Cam'ron kept his hands in his pockets the whole time as he watched Mr. Jerry with death in his eyes.

"So what you saying is that you ain't gonna pay the debt that you owed my Daddy?"

Jerry laughed as he reached over and grabbed a 40 ounce of Colt 45 off the table that sat in front of him.

I said what the fuck I said you little dusty motherfucker."

Cam'ron pulled the 38 Special from his pocket with the quickness like he'd seen on the quick draw cowboy movies.

"You gonna yet my money you fat motherfucker!"

Mr. Jerry's eyes grew wide as golf balls when Cam'ron cocked the hammer back just to let Mr. Jerry know he meant business. He got up off the couch and stepped through the sea of trash daring Mr. Jerry to move his fat ass one inch. He stepped to just out of Mr. Jerry's reach as Mr. Jerry started jeffing and raised his stinking arms up to show his hands like they did on t.v. when people were getting robbed or arrested.

Cam'ron could see the tracks on the man's arms and legs. The stains under his arm pits looked like someone had been pissin and shittin under his arms and smelled like it too.

"Aiight young'n! Aiiright! I got your money. I just gotta get it out the back room."

Cam'ron had been to the house when his father made his pickups, so he knew that Jerry kept everything in the back bedroom. He just didn't know if Jerry might try something.

Cam'ron took a step back so the fat bitch could get up. "Don't try no dumb shit! Now get my Daddy's money!"

Jerry put his hand on the side of the chair as if to push himself up and out of the chair. As he did, he tried to rush Cam'ron all in one motion to roll right over the little boy and overwhelm him. Cam'ron was caught off guard by the speed of the fat man and squeezed the trigger. Blaaaam!

The shot caught Jerry in the side, but his momentum carried him forward like a runaway train.

He hit Cam'ron and knocked him back off his feet into the couch arm rest. The crates holding the couch up collapsed as Jerry fell on top of Cam'ron's leg then slid down to the floor with a grunt like a stuck pig. The smell of hot beer mixed with all the other funk as Jerry dropped the 40 Ounce.

Cam'ron's leg screamed in agony from the weight of the man falling on him, as he saw stars for a minute. When his vision cleared, he looked down and saw Jerry crawling across the floor in the trash tryna get up and make it to the back room.

Cam'ron tried to stand, and his leg buckled as he did making him fall to the floor in agony. He watched Mr. Jerry reach and pull himself up leaving a bloody handprint on the hall's entryway.

Cam'ron fought the pain and hurried to get up. He realized he still had the gun, cocked it, and aimed before the man bent the corner.

"Blam! Blam! Blam!"

He got off three shots. The third one caught Jerry in the ass just as, he turned his way down the hall. Cam'ron heard his fat ass grunt as his shitty draws started turning red where he hit him.

The fat motherfucker kept moving even with two bullets in him. The fat was like armor on his ass and shooting someone wasn't as easy as it looked on t.v. since you had to get aim on a moving target.

By the third shot Cam'ron had his aim down, understood the kick of the gun, and how he needed to work it.

He limped over slipping a few times in all the trash and blood to peek down the hall. He could see the door was ajar, but couldn't see inside the room. He had two more bullets left and had to make em count.

As he made his way down the hall he heard heavy footsteps moving back toward the door and jumped back around the corner, just as he heard a Click-Clack, BOOOOM! From a shotgun.

The pellets sprayed just where he'd been standing and he would've been dead if he'd have been further down the hall.

He heard the fat man limp back down the hall talkin shit in his country drawl.

"I got da gun now nigga! Come on motherfucker! Come see da rabbit!"

He let off another shot down the hall trying to angle it back into the living room to intimidate Cam'ron. What he didn't know was that Cam'ron wasn't scared anymore. His heart was beating fast and he loved the rush of what he was facing. The gun in his hand was the only thing left to remind him of his father and he intended to use it well.

He waited until right when he heard Jerry go to pump the gun again, then rolled right out into the hall as he squeezed off.

Blam! Blam! Click! Click! Click!

He laid there and waited for Mr. Jerry to

return fire.

He didn't......

****

The first family Cam'ren was placed with were named the Jackson's. They were a black couple with a young daughter named Tammy that was just a few years older than Cam'ren.

She had bumps all over her face and wore pig tails with bright ribbons in her hair like she was a giant version of a black Barbie with bad skin.

She stayed in Cam'ren's face constantly and her breath turned Cam'ren's stomach every time she tried to kiss him. When she saw that wasn't working she tried to put the muscle down on him until he caught her one day and hit her to the body. Tammy crumpled and started crying. She threatened to tell her mother and father on him and not having any place to go kind of scared Cam'ren.

He begged Tammy not to tell on him and she promised not to, if he'd be her boyfriend. Cam'ren gave in although he wasn't feeling Tammy like that. She tried to kiss him and Cam'ren gave in just to keep her quiet.

Eventually, the kissing led to Tammy's hot ass extorting him to do all types of sexual favors. At night she would sneak into Cam'ren's room while her parents were asleep and climb into the bed to grind on Cam'ren in her little nighty.

Cam'ren had never actually had sex, so he tried to do what he'd seen his father doing and found out real fast that Tammy was a cold freak!

He started rubbing her through her sheer granny panties just the way he'd learned from watching his father, and Tammy soaked her panties as she panted all up in his face with her hot musty breath.

Then Cam'ren slid her wet panties to the side and stuck his finger inside of her and started moving it in and out real slow. Tammy clamped her legs down on his hands so tight, that at first he thought he had hurt Tammy and tried to jump up out of the bed.

Tammy wasn't having any of that and grabbed his ass back onto the bed so quick he thought he was in a wrestling match.

Tammy started pulling his pajama pants down as she straddled him and pulled his hard penis out. She looked at it and Cam'ren watched her as she started sucking on his dick like it was a blow pop. Cam'ren had never felt anything that felt as good as what she was doing to him. He just layed back and let her hot ass work.

Tammy came up for air and started rubbing all over his chest while trying to kiss him. Cam'ren wasn't havin it and turned his head to dodge her funky breath.

He felt Tammy reach between her legs and guide his young manhood inside her hot little box. At first there was resistance as she kept on trying to force him inside of her and it hurt

Cam'ren as his dick bent till it felt like she was gonna break him.

Just when he thought he couldn't take any more he felt something inside of her pop and he slid inside of her inch by inch.

Her young walls wrapped around him like a glove as she moved slowly at first all warm inside. Eventually Tammy got used to the sensation and moved faster and faster like she was slow grinding on him. She begged him, "Ooh Cam'ren! Suck my titty. Pleease suck my titty." As she picked up the pace and slapped her bony ass down faster and faster across his hips.

Her nappy pussy hairs burned and chafed him as she worked faster and faster.

Cam'ran reach up and pulled down her night gown to expose two perky breasts with dimes for nipples. He licked and sucked when he could reach them, as Tammy bounced so hard and fast he couldn't keep his lips on them for long.

This drove Tammy crazy and Cam'ren could feel her pussy muscle squeeze and release on his dick as the pussy got wetter and Tammy started shaking.

"OOOh Cammm'rrrrennnnn! I'm cooooom-mmmminnnng!"

Cam'ren tried to cover her mouth cause the dumb bitch was gettin too loud and he was scared she'd wake up her parents.

Just as he tried to cover her mouth he started feeling a tingling in his own balls that sent chills through his whole body. He felt his balls drop and fluid start rising up the base of his dick. Within seconds he was feeling his first orgasm right along with Tammy and he loved it! Now he looked at Tammy in a whole nother light. She was his first girlfriend and he was her first lover. From that moment on everything had changed. Tammy became Cam'ren's boss, mother, and girlfriend all rolled up into one. He did whatever she asked him to do and would fight anybody who messed with her.

That Tammy started trouble just to see him defend her was beyond Cam'ren's comprehendsion. He didn't see a bumpy faced twig with bad breath anymore. He was pussy whipped and Tammy controlled him.

One night she told him to come into her room while her parents slept. He wasn't going to turn her down the way she was sucking him off and sexing him real good.

He went to her room and they ended up doing the damn thing for about an hour.

He busted one nut and was going for his second when her parents busted into her room.

Mr. Jackson grabbed him in mid stroke and had to pull him off of Tammy with force because she was still trying to pull him inside of her by his ass.

Mr. Jackson snapped! "You gettin yo' ass out of here tonight! You going back to social services!" He yelled while pulling Cam'ren up by the throat.

Tammy kept trying to pull him back down.

"Stop Daddy! I love him!" She yelled over the loud commotion as balls of sweat rolled down the side of her face.

"You little freak bitch, you don't know shit bout no goddamn love. You ain't shit, but a freak like yo' hot assed Momma!" Mr. Jackson yelled as he looked down on his naked daughter while shaking his head.

Cam'ren was shocked at hearing the way her father talked down to her.

"I hate you!" Tammy cried while covering her body with her sheet.

"I don't give a fuck who you hate or love, this nigga is gettin outta here tonight!" He said dragging Cam'ren out of the bedroom.

Tammy just sat on the bed in a ball crying her eyes out about her father taking away her play thing. She also hoped that she wasn't pregnant after having sex with him so much without protection.

Cam'ren on the other hand was looking for a way outta there. Mr. Jackson knew what he was thinking and put him in his room with a chair up against the door so he couldn't get out of his room.

A few hours later Cam'ren saw that Mr. Jackson had stayed right in front of the door watching him the entire time while he slept.

The crazy thing about it was that the man had a nerve to have a can of mace in his hand like he intended to use it on Cam'ren if he tried to leave!

When Mr. Jackson noticed that Cam'ren was awake, he got up out of the chair with the can of Mace still in his hand like he was a prison guard. "Come on you little nasty motherfucker! Get yo ass up cause it's time ta go!"

"Shit," Cam'ren said under his breath.

Mr. Jackson just ignored him and called to his wife in the other room once he'd watched Cam'ren pack his shit and get dressed, "Baby I need you to drive while I sit in the back with him."

"Alright Honey," she said as she grabbed the car keys off of her dresser and made her way down the hall.

After Mr. Jackson let Cam'ren put his shoes on he held onto his arm as he walked him down the stairs and out the front door with his wife bringing up the rear.

Mr. Jackson put Cam'ren in the back seat then climbed in right next to him where he said he'd be.

Cam'ren couldn't have jumped out even if he wanted to.

Twenty minutes later they pulled up in front of the social services building.

Mr. Jackson had his eyes on Cam'ren the whole time as they got out of the car and headed inside of the building. When they got inside, Mrs. Jackson headed into Cam'ren's Social Worker's office while Mr. Jackson sat on the bench with Cam'ren.

Moments later Mrs. Jackson walked out with Mrs. White, the head of Social Services. She brought a guard along with her who presumably was to take over custody of Cam'ren from Mr. Jackson.

"You can come back with me Mr. Jackson. The officer will watch him."

Mr. Jackson headed into the back with Mrs. White while Cam'ren sat out on the bench for about an hour with the guard. When the Jacksons came out of the office with big smiles on their faces, Cam'ren was puzzled as he watched the Jackson's leave.

"You can bring Mr. Monday back!" Mrs. White said while looking at the guard.

As Cam'ren came into the small office of Mrs. White he didn't know what to expect. He sat down across from the elderly black woman and waited to see what would happen as she removed her old cat woman glasses that laid across her chest on a chain.

"Young man I don't know what your problem is, but you've ruined a very good opportunity for yourself. That was a good family! Now I don't have any place I can put you except in a group home."

Mrs. White continued to give him a piece of her mind until his ride finally arrived. Cam'ren didn't hear much of what she said since the old woman didn't intimidate him very much. He just tuned her out.

He stayed in the group home with a number

of other boys his age for only a few weeks before he was brought back down to the Social Services Building again.

When he was brought into Mrs. White's small office, a black man and white woman sat in the seat across from Mrs. White waiting on him.

They were a mixed couple named the Johnson's. Mrs. Johnson was a thick white woman in her mid-thirties. She was a pretty woman with long black hair. She stood about 5'7" and weighed about 143 pounds. When she turned her head to look to Mrs. White Cam'ren noticed that she also had blond streaks in her hair as highlights.

Mr. Johnson on the other hand was 6'2" with a slender build about himself. He had a bald head and a very disciplined look like a cop or a soldier.

They sat and got to know Cam'ren for a while and explained that they couldn't have children of their own. They explained that they couldn't take the place of his mother or father, but if he let them, they'd give him all the love they had.

Cam'ren couldn't believe it, but he had no place else to go. He didn't know where his brother was and had no one else to turn to. He agreed to give it a try.

They left social services after signing some paperwork. They took him to his new home, and as they pulled up to the house, Cam'ren fell in love with their 4 bedroom brick home immediately. When he discovered that they had a pool out back, they smiled at the pleasure Cam'ren showed.

Cam'ren knew that he could get used to the way these people lived. He just had to make sure he didn't screw it up and get kicked out again.

A few months later the Johnsons enrolled Cam'ren into a private school, but Cam'ren didn't want to go. He wanted to continue going to public school in the hopes that he could find out something about what had happened to his brother.

The Johnson's didn't understand, but relented and let him continue to attend the school he went to in Summerton South Carolina called Scott Branch.

****

Across town, Cam'ron was doing his own thing in the projects. Him and his friend Troy along with a few other young bucks from the projects started selling the heroin that Cam'ron had stolen from Mr. Jerry. Once he got himself established with a few flips of the heroin, Cam'ron bought a few more guns for his squad.

Gradually Cam'ron began to hit every motherfucker that owed his Pops money. If they didn't have his paper, he took their product. If they didn't have his product or the money, he took their life until he made a name for himself on the streets.

Cam'ron started running shit real heavy from his home base in the projects. The only person he trusted was Troy.

Him and Troy had hooked up when Cam'ron started dealing with an old head he got weight from named Tank. Tank lived across Santee Bring and always gave him good numbers on the weight he sold.

Cam'ron was 14 years old and was now getting more money than any of the older cats that had been out there for many years before him. He ended up supplying most of the older cats with work and all of them knew not to fuck with him since he was always ready to put in work with his squad.

It was like Cam'ron was born to ball. It was in his genes and what he didn't know, he learned real fast. You couldn't catch Cam'ron slippin, and if you didn't have that money right, him and his squad of young guns would be on your ass like flies on shit. So, nobody played any games with him.

He still kept wondering where his brother was, but the streets kept him focused. He was on a paper chase like he was obsessed since he didn't have anyone he could count on. There were moves to be made, and Cam'ron wanted to ball on the level that Gangsters Moved....

CHAPTER 5

Cam'ren settled into his life with Stephen and Karen Johnson. He did well in school and would often hear rumors about his brother.

Cam'ron didn't come to his school looking for him and Cam'ren didn't go getting in his brother's business.

In truth, Cam'ren felt that he had betrayed his brother by jumping at his first opportunity to leave him behind.

He knew his twins nature for trouble and just felt that with him around he would never be able to fulfill his dreams.

He didn't know if Cam'ron knew that Stephen and Karen Johnson had adopted him. He suspected that Cam'ron would not have liked it or the fact that he had his own hopes and aspirations that fell far beyond the criminal elements that he was hearing about concerning him.

He suspected that it all started when they were both young, since while Cam'ron longed to be a gangster like his father, Cam'ren always dreamed of being a cop.

To have been placed in a home where Mr. Johnson worked as a detective gave him all the opportunity he needed.

Stephen Johnson constantly drilled into Cam'ren the importance of staying away from negative influences so that he could be a legitimately successful black man rather than a thug.

When Stephen told him this, he knew right away that Cam'ron could never come around these people. Mr. Johnson would've locked him up at the first indication that he was involved in some of the murders that he'd personally investigated.

Cam'ren knew his brother and word was around he'd been involved in a number of killings. Cam'ren felt it was best that he stayed away from Cam'ron as much as possible.

He stayed out of trouble and made good grades so he'd have a chance to go to college.

When he did graduate, he graduated with honors and had been accepted at Howard University; the Alma Mater of Stephen Johnson. To be studying law on top of that brought even greater pride to the Johnson family.

The day he graduated from High School, Karen and Stephen Johnson were right there in the front row snapping pictures as happy as two parents could be.

Cam'ren missed his mother and his father. He would never forget either one of them, and in his mind he hoped his true mother Shirley was up in heaven very proud of him.

On his first day of college his mother wept as she sent him off to live on campus. They'd even given him a brand new 2003 CLK as a going away present. It was all good for Cam'ren.

When he got on grounds it took him a minute to find his way.

He drove around trying to find his dorm building and wound up getting lost.

He pulled over in front of a building that looked like it was a girl's fraternity to try to get someone's attention for directions.

"A yo! Excuse me ladies. Could you give the directions to dormitory number 12?"

A few of the girls sitting on the steps looked to see who he was. Cam'ren was clean in his new CLK.

What he didn't see was a black and Spanish chick come running up the walk in a pair of black leotards from behind him as he went to step out of the car.

The sister ran right into him since she couldn't stop in time.

She tried to skid and swerve around the door, but couldn't get out of the way fast enough. The sister tumbled so she wouldn't hit the door head on and twisted her ankle as she fell.

"Oh shit! I'm so sorry!" Cam'ren said as he stepped out of the car.

The chick looked hurt and was favoring her ankle.

When Cam'ren was able to stand her up he got a chance to get a good look at her.

Baby girl was fine as hell! She was 5'9" thick in all the right places, and obviously mixed with something Cam'ren couldn't quite place.

"It's okay! I shoulda been paying better attention. I'll be alright," she said as she started to limp down the walkway toward the girls he'd just asked for directions.

Since he still didn't know where he was going, he decided to ask her after checking out her ass. The black leotards she had on hugged her like a second skin and Cam'ren just couldn't let something that fine just limp away.

"Here, let me help you," he said as he grabbed her elbow to lead her towards the steps.

She smiled in gratitude, "Thanks, it seems you're my knight in shining armor now."

"Naw, it was my fault. I've got too many boxes behind me, so I couldn't see you coming."

The sister looked back and noticed that it looked like Cam'ren was moving. "Oh! You just got here! I'm sorry, my name is Nancy."

Cam'ren shook her hand. "I'm Cam'ren. I'm just trying to find my dorm."

They both stopped in front of the steps as the four women out on the porch watched their sorority sister and Cam'ren talking.

You could tell that they were jealous as hell after getting a better look at Cam'ren now.

One fat chick with long dreads jumped into the conversation. "Excuse me. Didn't you just ask "us" for directions?"

Cam'ren looked back at Nancy then back at the fat chick with the dreads, "I think I've found them."

She rolled her eyes at him and turned to finish talking to her friend with an attitude.

Nancy whispered to Cam'ren, "Excuse my sister. She's a cock blocker anyway."

The fat chick heard her and Cam'ren could tell there was about to be tension, so he wanted to pull up. "Well can you tell me where building 12 is?"

Nancy gave him directions and waved goodbye before going up the steps to have a talk with the fat chick that Cam'ren didn't want to hear. He'd be seeing her again on campus. Now just wasn't the time.

At his first class, there she was just three rows in front of him. Nancy was a first year law student just like him. Cam'ren could see as she left the class that Nancy had the looks of Tyra Banks and the body to match. Everything on her body was Gucci and Prada. That told Cam'ren that her family had money! She wasn't wearing no cheap shit.

She waved as she passed Cam'ren on her way up the aisle to go out of class. Cam'ren got up to say hello.

"How's your ankle doing?"

"I hope I didn't get you into anything the other day."

Nancy smiled, "Naw, it's okay. That bitch was just jealous."

"I thought sorority girls were supposed to be sisters."

Nancy gave him a "be serious" look. "Listen,

just cause we in a sorority together doesn't mean that we have to like each other."

Cam'ren could relate to that. That was what Stephen and Karen tried to instill in him his whole life growing up.

"I can relate to that. But why don't we talk about it some other time. Like tonight?"

Nancy giggled and agreed to meet him at the library around 7:00.

Cam'ren couldn't wait. He jetted back to his dorm and tried to finish the last little bit of unpacking, then hit the books to start familiarizing himself with the curriculum.

At 6:00 he got up and got clean. He didn't want Nancy thinking he slouched in the gear department. He wasn't the richest, but his parents made sure he had the best!

He stepped out and watched as everyone moved to and from their final classes or talked about the coming year of study. The campus was in a party atmosphere. Everyone was getting to know everybody. Cam'ren had already met everyone on his floor, so he knew it was on and popping for the night. Their dorm was supposed to be having a keg party. His plan was to see if Nancy wanted to go.

When he pulled up, Nancy was standing there waiting for him. She looked good as hell in a tight pair of faded denim jeans with a light leather jacket. Her hair hung back in a ponytail with curls flowing down her back.

Cam'ren's mouth started watering the

better the view he got. The green cashmere sweater Nancy wore made her breasts sit up like two perfectly sized mangos. She had on a gold chain with a small diamond cross that sat nestled between her breasts.

This attracted Cam'ren even more since he felt that Nancy would be just the type of chick that he needed. She had that wholesome wifey look that every man desires and the books that she was carrying only made her more attractive to Cam'ren.

When he met her on the steps she smiled and it was like her eyes lit up everything around her. Cam'ren was really feeling this girl.

"So what's up for tonight?" She asked as they turned to head back to his car.

"I wanted to see if you'd be interested in coming to my dorm's party after we had something to eat."

Nancy didn't appear put off by the idea and Cam'ren was glad for that.

"Where we gonna eat first?"

Cam'ren didn't want to take her to the regular cafeteria.

That wouldn't have impressed a girl like Nancy at all.

"How bout you pick since I'm new here." He said as he opened his car door.

Nancy thought for a minute, then said okay.

She gave him directions to a quaint little restaurant in the city. The place looked expensive and Cam'ren hoped he didn't have to start using his parent's credit card already since he wasn't rich.

He soon found out that Nancy had "very" expensive tastes.

When they sat down to order, Nancy ordered for both of them then started talking about her life.

Both her parents were corporate executives. She didn't come to Howard on a scholarship. Her parents paid her full tuition.
She had a second apartment off campus as well as a room paid for in the Sorority house.

The food came and each of them got more comfortable as they ate. Cam'ren told her about his father working in Law Enforcement and how he was considering work as either a prosecutor or private attorney.

When they were done eating, the bill was high as shit. Cam'ren didn't say anything about it. He also made sure he left a nice tip. He'd worry about his father cussing him out for it later. Tonight, he wanted to impress Nancy.

On the ride back to the dorm the vibe was great. Their conversation pretty much revolved around some of the same classes that they shared and the coming curriculum. It was easy to find a lot of things that they had in common.

Cam'ren pulled up to his dorm and could see that the party was just gettin started. Music thumped from open windows as many of his dorm mate's friends arrived. Some people were drunk already.

Many of the guys seemed to all know Nancy. Cam'ren assumed that it was because she was a popular girl in the sorority.

When they made their way into the main room they both got real comfortable. They danced and Cam'ren enjoyed the opportunity to watch Nancy's nice body in motion. Pretty soon they were both sweating and a little tipsy.

Beer flowed freely from kegs all over the room and every few songs he and Nancy had a few drinks.

Cam'ren just knew he had a dream chick. She was pretty, smart, well off, and could hang in a party atmosphere.

As the party started to make its way into the late hours, he and Nancy made their way to Cam'ren's room. They were both pretty tired and feeling good.

When Cam'ren turned to shut the door behind him, Nancy was right there in his face. Cam'ren wasn't sure if it would've been premature to try and kiss her since thy hardly knew each other. Nancy made up his mind for him.

She kissed Cam'ren passionately. Even with beer breath her mouth tasted good.

Cam'ren pushed her back against the wall and Nancy drooped her small Gucci purse on the floor to hug him.

Cam'ren began to slow grind up on Nancy against the door as they continued their kiss.

Nancy pushed Cam'ren back a step.

"Woe, woe, let's slow down," she said as they both caught their breath.

Cam'ren was embarrassed slightly since he hadn't had a lot of interaction with females after the incident with Tammy.

"My bad Nancy. I'm just feeling you," he said as he tried to cover his hard on.

Nancy looked down with a smirk on her face at his trying to cover his bulging pants.

"I was feeling you too!"

They both laughed then Nancy took control again. She took off Cam'ren's shirt and started undressing him as they started kissing again.

In turn, Cam'ren helped her with her jacket then lifted off her sweater to expose a Victoria's Secret bra. He could see she had on a matching thong tied over her hips that had been covered by the sweater.

Together they got her out of her tight jeans, then made their way to his bed.

Nancy laid back on the small mattress and looked up at Cam'ren with a smile, "I hope you don't think I do this all the time."

"It's been a long time for me too," Cam'ren responded as he bent down to kiss her.

Nancy stopped him, "Do you have protection?"

Cam'ren reached under the mattress and pulled out a row of Magnums. Nancy smiled and helped him put it on. When she was done she climbed on top of him and grabbed hold of the head board as she slid down his rock hard shaft.

The pussy was good to Cam'ren. He could feel her stomach as she dropped down on the low ride tip.

Gradually she began to pick up the pace and started riding Cam'ren like a professional jockey.

Cam'ren bust a nut almost immediately from the intensity of how she was fucking him.

Nancy climbed off and switched to a fresh condom like a pro. Before Cam'ren knew what hit him, Nancy had him hard again and hitting it from the back, then legs over the shoulders.

After he came again, Nancy went down and gave him some head to keep him hard. Before he knew what was going on she spun around on top of him into a 69 position and had her pussy in his face.

Cam'ren had never eaten pussy before. The only inkling he had was when he'd seen his father get killed.

He tried to blank out that image and work as he'd seen his father do. It seemed to please Nancy as he enjoyed exploring her insides.

Nancy started working her hips guiding his tongue repositioning her hips to all of her special places until she gave Cam'ren his first Santa Claus face when she came in his mouth.

Cam'ren received as good as he got and in minutes he came himself.

When they wore done, they lay snuggled up in Cam'ren's dorm room bed with Cam'ren wondering if they were a couple now.

****

Cam'ren and Nancy became almost inseparable as an item. They both loved the same things, sex and law. She wanted to be a District Attorney one day, and even convinced Cam'ren to consider applying to the F.B.I. for a job in their final year before the bar. Things were going great.

One day as Cam'ren sat studying for finals, Nancy his dorm room as she usually did--without knocking.

Cam'ren had his eyes glued to the computer screen kissed the nape of his neck sending chills throughout Nancy had Cam'ren turned out as a set addict. She was like a nympho who had to have it two and three times a day!

"So what's up Baby?" She asked while rubbing his shoulders.

Cam'ren was exhausted. He'd been studying for hours and really didn't have the energy to wrestle with Nancy. In truth, it was getting kind of boring since all they did was fuck; and study. That didn't mean she didn't drive him crazy every time she touched him.

Just her massaging his shoulders at that moment was making him hard. He just had to study for his exams.

"Baby we've got a huge exam in a couple of weeks. I really need to study for this if I'm going to pass!" He said.

Nancy gave him the pouting face and kept on massaging him trying to keep him aroused.

Cam'ren tried to ignore her as she started rubbing down onto his chest. Cam'ren couldn't concentrate.

"You know if you keep doing what you're doing you're going to start something."

Nancy giggled, "I know, that's what I want!"

Cam'ren shook his head frustrated. He'd been slacking in his studies for weeks because of Nancy's nympho tendencies. He didn't know where she got the energy from. Cam'ren was just tired of her.

He turned around in his chair and took her hands out of his shirt while he looked up at her.

"Nancy, listen to me for a second. I want to be able to pass the bar. Not everybody that comes from where I come from gets the chances that I've been given. My family isn't wealthy like yours.

I've got the chance to be part of one of the greatest Law enforcement agencies on the planet. This is my dream. It's everything that my family and I have worked for. So I need to study."

Nancy crossed her arms and wasn't really tryna hear what Cam'ren was telling her.

"Quit being a bore!" She said with exasperation.

Cam'ron couldn't seem to get through to her. He kept pulling anyway.

"Look, where I come from you have to try your hardest or you'll be on the other side of the justice system. Most of the guys I grew up with are either dead, strung out on dope, or locked up. Very few of them have had the chances I've had to go to college. I don't wanna be like that."

What he really meant was that he didn't want to be like his twin brother.

Nancy screwed up her face like she was irritated. "Oh, so now you're saying that I didn't come from the hood. Is that what you're trying to say?"

Cam'ren just shook his head in frustration.

I'm not saying that. I'm just saying that I lost both of my parents. I don't know what happened to my twin brother when my father got killed. Plus, my mother died of cancer when I was a baby. I had to live in a foster home for a while, and if it wasn't for my adopted family I would've been just like the rest of the guys I grew up with. Now what do you know about that?"

Nancy stood there surprised.

"I'm sorry Boo, I didn't know you'd been through all of that."

"I know, but I don't like talking about that kind of stuff. It's depressing."

Nancy nodded her understanding, then perked up. "Wanna go out for dinner tonight? My treat!"

Cam'ren laughed appreciating the gesture. "Alright, just let me get through a few more pages. Then we can hit the town."

Nancy jumped over and planted a juicy kiss on Cam'ren then sashayed to the door. Before she left she turned, "I'm going back to the Sorority House to handle a few things. What time will I see you?"

"I should be done at about 7:00, so I'll stop by at about 7:30."

"Okay, I'll be nice and fresh for you," she said as she shook her ass a little extra on the way out the door.

"That girl is really shot out!" Cam'ren said as he turned back to do some more studying.

After finishing a few more pages, he realized that he wasn't getting anywhere. He decided to wrap up early.

He washed up, put on his cream colored Polo outfit with matching Polo sneakers that he'd just picked up a few days ago on Georgetown Avenue.

He even threw on a little Polo Muslim oil to seal the deal. He looked into his full length mirror and just knew he was the shit.

His dread locks hung down to his shoulders, and for a split second, wondered if he looked more like his mother or his father.

Expressing so much of what he'd kept bottled in made him miss both of his real parents a great deal.

He'd done the best he could not to live the life that his father had. He didn't want that to be his fate. 'He only hoped that his brother wouldn't end up like his father had, living the lifestyle that he'd heard he was leading.

At the same time, he considered his relationship with Nancy. He'd finally opened up on a more personal level with her that went beyond sex and wondered if he was actually in love with her.

He enjoyed the time spent with her and could see them possibly getting married and becoming a team like his adopted parents. He'd just have to see how things worked out.

Cam'ren closed down his computer and headed out the door. He jumped in his 2003 CLK and headed over to Nancy's Sorority house.

When he got there the fat chick with the dread locks named Sandra that he ran into the first day he arrived on campus was sitting out front.

"Heyyy Cam'ren. Damn, you look good! Do Nancy know you coming over?" She said sarcastically. Cam'ren didn't get why she hated Nancy so much.

"I'm a little bit early tonight," he said as he checked his watch and realized it was only 6:30. "Can you let her know I'm here?"

The sister just laughed like she knew something he didn't. "Naw, you can go right up to her room. I think she said she was waitin on you."

With that, Cam'ren made his way up the stairs and to Nancy's room. He wanted to surprise her since he had finished up early.

He didn't even knock.

As he opened the door he heard loud music playing and assumed she was in her room grooving while she got ready.

When he opened the door all the lights were out and there was a strong smell of sex in the air.

Cam'ren reached over and turned on the lights and for a minute thought he'd come to the wrong room. It took him a minute to realize that who he saw and what he saw was real.

Nancy was on the bed with her eyes shut and two dicks in her mouth sucking like there was no tomorrow. As he took in the whole scene he realized that another dude was behind his woman hitting her from the back doggy style.

All three of the men froze when they saw Cam'ren in the doorway.

Nancy's eyes popped open to see why they'd stopped and realized it was Cam'ren who was standing in the doorway.

"Oh my God!" She mumbled with dick still stuck in her mouth. She jumped off the bed and tried to rush over to grab Cam'ren's arm.

Cam'ren pulled away from her. "Bitch! Get yo' triflin hands off me before I kill you!"

Cam'ren turned to walk out the door and saw the fat chick with the dread locks laughing hysterically down the hall. Cam'ren understood now why Nancy was so popular and all of the sorority brothers seemed to know her. He recognized the dude's gang banging her as being from her brother frat. She was a closet freak and only pretended to be Mrs. Innocent for him.

Cam'ren brushed by the fat chick and kept it movin. He could hear her behind him. "Now you know who that bitch really is" and started laughing even harder.

Outside Cam'ren jumped into his car and

headed onto Georgetown Avenue trying to get a grip on what he'd just seen. He spotted a bar along the way and pulled over into its parking lot.

He jumped out and headed inside to get a drink and try to calm down.

The place was smokey and filled with hustlers, pimps, and drug dealers. He paid them no mind as he stepped up to the bar and ordered himself a drink.

He drank shot after shot of Patrone until the pain of what he'd just experienced became a blur in his memory. As he finished up his fourth shot he felt a hand on his shoulder. When he turned around, he saw a sexy sister sporting a cat suit that showed every inch of her well-proportioned body.

"Are you buying?" She asked with a seductive smile on her pretty face.

Cam'ren smiled as he tried to focus on her erect nipples showing through her tight suit. "Order whatever you want Shorty, it's on me."

The sister flagged the bartender over ordered a shot for herself, then turned to introduce herself. "By the way, my name is Sunshine."

Cam'ren introduced himself and Sunshine purred like a kitten.

"Ooh! That is a sexy name! Let's get out of here and have us a little party of our own."

Cam'ren couldn't have said it better himself. They both left together after finishing their drinks.

****

Later on that night at the Motel 6.

"Oh shit, right there baby. Beat this pussy up like you love it! I want to feel you deeper inside of me!" Sunshine barked in a moan like voice as Cam'ren pounded away at her guts.

Sunshine reached around and started massaging his nut sack until he climaxed like he never had with Nancy.

The next day he woke up to Sunshine's hot mouth around his rock hard morning member. She looked up into his sleep encrusted eyes as she deep throated him to the bone. Cam'ren grabbed the top of her head and began to guide her as he made love to her face.

His head was killing him from the night before, but the way she was blowing him took all of that away and brought back pure pleasure between his thighs.

CHAPTER 6

In South Carolina, Cam'ron and one of his squad named Smash stood in front of his BBQ Restaurant. He'd bought it a few years back and now had his homie Boog running it as a legitimate business.

They watched a few local hustlers making their transactions up the street from the restaurant as they shot the breeze.

Smash was his number one dude even though he had a small man's complex. Smash stood around 5'4" at 150 pounds, and always kept a gun in his waist.

He had a thing for going at big jokers to prove himself. Most of the dudes he went at learned real fast how dangerous he was and tried to steer clear of him. Everybody in the small town of Summerton learned that to mess with Smash meant you could end up dead and stinking in the Santee River.

Cam'ron was way up in the game. He'd just bought a mansion for 1.5 million that sat on 3,400 acres of land.

He had a swimming pool built in the back yard with his face painted on the bottom.

He had a landscaper come out and put Palm Trees all around the property as though it was built in Miami instead of South Carolina.

Cam'ron had his dark blue Tahoe truck sitting on 24's in the driveway of the restaurant with Ghetto boys playing as they talked. "This year Halloween fell on a weekend, me & Ghetto Boys went trick or treating!" Could be heard nearly a mile away from his system.

He also had his 1969 Impala sitting in the grass on the other side of the BBQ joint.

As they took in the scenery and talked for another 30 minutes, they noticed a white Lexus with grey stripes on the side pull up onto the property.

They stopped their conversation and focused on the car since they didn't recognize it.

The Lexus stopped right in front of them and a white woman got out of the passenger's side door. A black bald man climbed out of the driver's side and started walking towards them.

Cam'ron didn't know if he should stand there or take off. He knew it was his restaurant, but he'd never seen these people before.
He thought they might have been the feds since the bald guy carried a gun on his hip.

As the two approached he noticed that each of them were smiling at him in particular as if they knew him.

The white woman spoke first, "Hey Honey, when did you get back into town?"

"Do I know you people" Cam'ron asked with a confused look.

"Boy stop playing!" Stated the bald black

guy.

Cam'ron thought the couple was trippin for real! "Do it look as if I'm playing? I don't know you people from Adam," he said opening his eyes wide.

"Boy we're your damn parents!" Stated the black man.

"Excuse me sir, both my parents died a long time ago!" Cam'ron answered with his face broken up. He didn't know if these people were trying to play mind games. He looked over at Smash ready to give the signal for him to move out if they got crazy.

"Cam'ren, if you don't stop playing this very instant and come give your mother a hug, I'm going to come over there and pull you by those big ears of yours!" Stated Mrs. Johnson with her cheeks turning dark red now.

At hearing his brother's name, Cam'ron thought he knew what was going on.

"Excuse me Miss, Cam'ren is my brother's name, I'm Cam'ron."

"Your brother?" Mrs. Johnson asked looking at Cam'ron incredulously. She then pulled out her cell phone and started dialing Cam'ren's number.

The first try went straight to voice mail. She swallowed real hard trying to take everything in.

"Could Cam'ren have a twin brother and not have told us?" Was the look the Johnsons both shared with each other.

Mrs. Johnson tried Cam'ren's number a

second time.

"Hello?" Said a groggy Cam'ren.

When Mrs. Johnson heard her son's voice she swallowed real hard as she looked at Cam'ron who was standing directly in front of her.

She didn't know what to say.

"Hello! Helllooo! I can hear you breathing Nancy I know that it's you!" He yelled into the telephone.

That broke Cam'ren's mother out of her condition as she tried to answer Cam'ren.

"Cam'ren, this is your mother!" She said as she still kept an eye on Cam'ron.

"Hey Mom, what's up?" Cam'ren answered trying to recover some dignity. It was a lot harder since Sunshine kept moving her head up and down on his hammer.

"Boy, do you know that the craziest thing just happened to me and your father today?"

"Oh shit!" He moaned.

Mrs. Johnson was shocked at what she heard on the other end of the line from her son.

"What did you just say?"

"Oh nothing Mom, I just stumped my toe while I was talking to you. Now what happened to you and Dad today?" He asked between clenched teeth while trying not to moan out from the good head he was getting.

"Why didn't you tell me you had a brother? A twin at that!"

Cam'ren almost jumped out of the bed with

Sunshine stuck to him.

"What? How did you find out about that?"

"Because I'm standing right in front of him!"

Stephen and I were just riding through town and saw someone we thought was you. Come to find out, it is your twin brother."

Cam'ren didn't know how to react. He wanted to see his brother. He just couldn't believe the way that it was happening.

"Where is he now?"

"He's standing right here in front of us."

"Well put him on Ma. I want to talk to him."

She paused a moment and then handed Cam'ron the phone.

"Here, he wants to talk to you."

"Hello," stated Cam'ron after taking the phone.

"Cam'ron is that really you?" Cam'ren asked excitedly.

"No, the question is, is that really you?" Cam'ron shot back.

"Yeah it's really me. Why haven't you tried to find me?"

"The same reason you didn't try to find me?" Cam'ron shot back excited to have finally found his brother.

"Man I searched everywhere for you. I even went online trying to find you. It was like you'd vanished off the face of the earth or something."

Cam'ron laughed. "Well I'm here now and I've done good for myself."

"So what are you into bro?"

"Man I'm into big business. We're standing in front of one of my restaurants right now!"

"So when can we hook up?" Asked Cam'ren.

"When do you yet back in town?"

Cam'ren was kinda puzzled. "How do you know I'm not in town?"

"Because your mother asked me when I got back in town when she walked up on me. It ain't hard to tell."

"Well, I guess your right about that. See, I'm in college right now, but it's almost the end of the semester, maybe next month we could get together unless you wanna come up here for homecoming.

"When does that start?" Cam'ren asked as he looked over at Smash.

"It starts the beginning of next week. Can you make it?"

"Well, I can head out that way tonight!"

"Bet! Put my mother back on the phone."

"Alright Bro, here she goes."

Cam'ron didn't like that he was calling this white woman his mother. He didn't care if she raised Cam'ren or not. He tried not to let it show as he gave Mrs. Johnson her phone back.

They all said their goodbyes. The Johnson's jumped back into their car after exchanging information.

Cam'ron's mind was clicking on all four cylinders. He started coming up with big plans for the college campus. He couldn't help himself.

If it didn't make dollars it didn't make sense. He just had to feel his brother out to see if he was with it.

The first thing he had to do was go holler at his Old head Tank. It was almost time to re-up again and he wanted to handle that business before he left. He also had to get with his old lady Pam and make sure that she held down all the other legitimate businesses he now owned.

Once Cam'ron turned 18 he fixed and sold his parent's house. He bought more properties and went from there.

After he'd gotten the hang of doing legitimate business, he started using those businesses to clean the drug money he had coming in.

As time progressed and he and his girlfriend Pam had gotten closer, he moved in with her and her mother.

He paid all the bills so Pam's mother let him stay there with open arms.

With all the money he was making, he could pretty much do whatever he wanted. Now that he'd fulfilled his dream of owning a mansion he moved Pam and her mother in with him to return the favor.

Pam's mother still kept her house while Pam's mother Gina became a realtor investing his money in other property ventures. He paid Gina to run the company for him. Pam pretty much answered the phones and took care of the home front while he did his dirt on the side.

"Smash! Come on. Let's bounce. We have to handle this business before we roll out tonight," he said while heading for the driver's side of his truck.

Smash jumped into the passenger seat after fixing his gun on his waist line. They pulled out of the driveway and headed to their stash house. Cam'ron needed to pick up some money before heading across the river to re-up on work. As he headed up the road he noticed a car pulled over on the side of the road with a flat tire.

They both noticed the fat ass of the woman bending down on the other side of the car.

The only thing that Cam'ron and Smash were "really" focused on "was" the ass.

They could also see that she didn't have on any panties. That was most definitely the signal for Cam'ron to pull over. Cam'ron pulled in front of the car and turned to Smash.

"Yo', stay in the truck. I got this one." Cam'ron said while looking through the rear view mirror to make sure no traffic was coming before he got out.

Once everything was clear, he stepped out of his truck. The woman looked up and saw him coming in her direction. She watched as Cam'ron moved his long dreads from over his eyes before coming her way.

"Excuse me sexy! Do you need a hand with that tire?" He asked looking into her hazel eyes. She looked familiar to him once he got a chance to get a look at her. He just couldn't place where he must have known her from.

"Yes! I can't change a tire worth nothing!"

She said while wiping sweat from the side of her temple.

"Well where your man at? I know somebody as sexy as yo'self has to have a man at home waiting on you."

"What man?" She asked before standing up to give Cam'ron a better view of her body."

The only thing Cam'ron could think was, "Fuck Apple Bottom jeans. They should make Pumpkin Bottom for the ass she got!"

He knew Smash had to be looking. He turned and looked back to see that he was right. Smash was indeed looking, so he winked at him and looked down at the woman's rear.

"So you ain't got no man?" He asked, giving her a plus for that.

"Nope, its just me and my little sister," she said while putting her hands on her slender waist and leaning back on her bowed legs.

"So you got a sister huh? How old is she?"

"Oh, so now you want my sister? Anyway, she's 33!" She said eying her new candy.

Cam'ron thought about the age difference. He needed something older in his stable. Age wasn't nothing but a number to him. He didn't know how Smash felt. If her sister was as fine as she was, he knew Smash would see her as fair game.

He changed her tire and continued the conversation.

"So what's yo' name shorty?" He asked as he wiped the sweat off his brows and then brushed the dirt off."

"Alize!"

"Damn! That's a sexy damn name!"

"Do you want to follow me to my house?" She asked with one of her best smiles.

"Well, I'm kinda in a hurry right now. Just give me your number and we can hook up in the near future.

"That's what's up. Here's my number!" She said grabbing his phone and putting her number inside.

He looked at the number when he got the phone back, tucked it away, then got ready to step off.

"I'll get at you soon!" He said as he started heading back to his truck.

"You better!" She yelled after him.

Cam'ron turned back, "Don't worry, I got you Ma," then walked off with a little bop to his step.

He jumped inside his truck seconds later and gave Smash some dap before pulling off.

****

Cam'ron pulled into the driveway of his stash spot off Main Street. Troy ran the operation and oversaw all the accounting of the money in Cam'ron's stash. The only thing Cam'ron had to do was collect the money.

Cam'ron and Smash stepped out of Cam'ron's truck and headed for the front door. They walked up the limestone steps and Cam'ron knocked on the door using their code.

Like magic the door opened. Lil Shamrock stood on the other side with his dread locks hanging everywhere and a gold toothed smile.

You couldn't tell him that he wasn't a Rastafarian. Shamrock wore the clothes of a Rasta and rocked their music 24/7. He even tried to speak like them.

On top of that, you could smell the weed he was smoking as soon as you walked through the front door.

"What's up my dude?" Shamrock asked before giving Cam'ron some dap.

"Ain't shit baby, just tryna live!"

Shamrock nodded in agreement. "That's what I'm talkin bout! Smash, what up homie?"

Shamrock gave up the greetings as they both stepped in and checked out the scenery. Seeing that everything was in order, Cam'ron inquired about Troy.

"Where that niggah Troy at?"

"In the kitchen, doing what he do best!"

"I guess that's nothing!" Cam'ron said with a wide smile.

"You crazy man!" Shamrock shot back before putting the deadbolt on the front door as he shook his head.

Cam'ron made his way to the kitchen. Troy was sitting there counting stacks of money and smoking a dutch filled with Sour Dizzle.

"Yo! Pass that shit My Dude!" Cam'ron said from the entrance way of the kitchen.

Troy jumped as he dropped the money losing count.

"Damn Yo! Why you always do that shit? Now I gotta start all over again!"

Money covered the huge kitchen table in stacks. A counting machine clicked to a halt and beeped waiting to be refilled.

Along the wall were four duffel bags filled with money in Saran wrapped bricks for transport.

To the side of Troy hung an arsenal on the wall. There was hardly any room to maneuver in the cash filled kitchen.

Troy got up, adjusted his bullet proof vest and slid out of his chair to give Cam'ron some love.

When they were done their greetings, they each sat continuing to count the money.

Cam'ron got up to take a break and stretch his back after an hour or so.

"Yo! I got the best news today."

Troy leaned back and blew smoke from the puff he'd just taken from the Sour Dizzle.

"I talked to my brother today."

Troy started nodding his head as he exhaled, "Word my dude. Das what's up?"

"He wants me to come down there this week for their Homecoming at Howard University."

"You know what I'm thinking?" Troy asked

with the same look that Cam'ron had earlier.

They both bust out laughing on some ESP, "My mind was already there shit!"

Cam'ron quickly gave Troy a breakdown about his traveling plans. When he was done, they both looked at the money they'd just finished counting and agreed it was a plan.

Cam'ron zipped the last bag. Cam'ron hefted two of the duffel bags up on his shoulder after he strapped up.

"Let's make this happen" was all that needed to be said as they stepped towards the door.

Cam'ron and Smash loaded the other duffel bags into the Tahoe.

Cam'ron didn't like to be up in his stash spot for too long. There was always a possibility the police would run up on him. They headed over to Cam'ron's crib.

They pulled up to the black steel gates of Cam'ron's estate. Cam'ron pushed in a few numbers and the gate came open.

They pulled inside and parked next to Cam'ron's Bentley GT. They each jumped out and carried the duffel bags full of money into Cam'ron's garage, then stashed the duffel bags in a floor panel Cam'ron had built beneath the garage.

He kept an arsenal of weapons hidden there and out on his firing range in the back of his house.

He fed his stable of Pit Bull mastiffs, then

they made their way into the house.

They both headed straight for the kitchen to raid the refrigerator.

Cam'ron's wife Pam came down the back oval steps that led into the kitchen. You know! The kind they had on the Different Strokes show.

She looked and saw Smash all up in her fried chicken that she'd cooked for Cam'ron the night before.

"Boy! If you don't get them damn nasty hands of yours out of my shit!" She barked as she rolled her head with her hands on her hips. "Come on Pam wit all dat shit der girl!" Smash responded with a drumstick hangin off his lips.

Pam wasn't havin it.

"What you need to do is take your ass over to one of yo' chicken heads houses and bum rush de' shit wit yo' old greedy ass!" Pam responded.

Smash kept eating as he closed the kitchen door.

Cam'ron walked into the kitchen to see what was going on.

"Yo' my dude, check yo' woman!" Smash hollered at Cam'ron.

Cam'ron ignored him and headed straight up behind Pam. He hugged her from behind, then looked at Smash.

"Naw Man. She aiight!"

Pam started grinding her plump ass back against Cam'ron as she reached behind herself to give Cam'ron a hello kiss.

When they stopped she looked spitefully at

Smash.

"Ooh! You know das my spot rite dar!"

Cam'ron winked over at Smash and they both started laughing.

Smash rolled out with the bowl of chicken in hand so that Cam'ron and Pam could have a talk.

"Look Baby, we're about to head out of town for a few days." Cam'ron said as he started grinding on Pam's ass again. They were alone and he had to set things straight with her.

Pam balled her face right up and caught an attitude.

"How long you gonna be gone this time?!?"

"I'll be gone just a few days." Cam'ron responded as he kissed her on the neck.

Pam crossed her arms, cocked her hip, and screwed up her face like, "Yeah right!"

"I know what you said through dat hole in yo' face, but that ain't telling me shit!"

Cam'ron backed up off of her.

"Pam, I don't really know how long I'ma be gone. It could be one, two, three, or even four days! I'm going outta town to hook up with my brother."

Pam turned around and looked at Cam'ron like he was crazy.

What you say? Your brother?"

Cam'ron put his hands up smiling, "Yeah, I talked to him today!"

Pam just looked at him with the, "You better not be lying look."

Cam'ron kept smiling, "Real talk girl! I'm serious!"

Pam wasn't certain. She really didn't know a whole lot about Cam'ron's past or his family.

Finally, she started to believe, but just in case she warned him.

"It better only be your brother you goin to see! The last time you went to see somebody I got a damn STD!"

Cam'ron was hurt. "Aw go head girl wit all dat! That was the first and the last time I cheated on you!"

Pam knew better. She didn't complain because Cam'ron was in the game. She just wanted to be safe with Cam'ron and all Cam'ron thought about was the money.

She knew he cared about her. It was just that it seemed as if they only had a life revolving around him.

Pam needed more than just that.

Pam knew Cam'ron probably had about three kids that "she" could count. Cam'ron didn't know that she knew. But she kept track of his ass.

When Pam realized that Cam'ron wouldn't be faithful, she put together some secrets of her own.....

Cam'ron was too blind to see how she acted around his homie Troy. Whenever Troy was there and she came in the room, Troy would get up and leave.

They'd been creeping for more than a year

now and Pam was still tryna make up her mind about how to handle the results of that!

She was 5 weeks pregnant and didn't know which one of them were her baby's father.

Pam felt that the best thing to do would be to get rid of the baby.

Especially since if Cam'ron found out that she was cheating on him, "AND" was pregnant, both of them would be found dead and stinkin in the Santee Bring River."

The man had already killed people that she had personal knowledge of.

Later on, as she thought about this, Cam'ron came down the front steps with that shit on!

In each hand he carried leather LV luggage. The luggage was stuffed with Gucci, Polo, Versace, and other high priced designers. "Come on My Dude! We need to head over to Avis to get something nice to drive," he said as he went to open the door.

Pam climbed off the couch and came into the foyer.

She leaned up in the living room doorway looking.

"Damn, you can't give your future wife a goodbye kiss befo' you leave!"

Cam'ron dug himself. "Oh Shit!"

He backstepped away from the door to give Pam a kiss while ignoring the future wife shit.

Cam'ron looked at his partner as he opened the door, "Let's show these D.C. motherfuckers how Down South do it! Ya heard!" Then he walked out the door leaving Pam heated behind him.

CHAPTER 7

Cam'ren sat in his dorm back in D.C.

After talking to his brother, his whole day was "good".

To have Sunshine there sexin him the way that she was made his day even better.

He looked over towards Sunshine. She lay under his silk sheets snoring lightly.

He was tired too after what they'd been up to.

Having sex with Sunshine put a smile on his face. After Nancy, Sunshine brought new meaning to his life.

He wanted to wake up to her beautiful face every day and he couldn't believe how he was falling in love with her so quickly.
He also couldn't wait to see his brother after their being apart for so long.

He planned on introducing him to all of his friends on campus.

Sunshine rolled over to look at him as he leaned back on the headboard of the bed.

He rubbed her back and smiled. "Baby,you want me to get you something to eat?"

"Sure Boo! I'm starving." She answered as she tucked her head under his covers so he wouldn't smell her morning breath.

What she failed to tell him in the short time that they'd spent together was that she was a stripper and a prostitute at Club Butterfly from time to time.

She had a pimp named Ross and she was surprised that none of the men on campus noticed her.

She'd been in his room the entire time since they'd left the bar.

It was only a matter of time before somebody told Ross who she'd left the bar with.

Cam'ren kissed her on the forehead and headed out the door.

As soon as Cam'ren left, Sunshine jumped up out of the bed and called Ross on the phone.

"Yeah!" Ross barked through the line when he picked up.

"Hey Daddy, it's me."

"Bitch! Where the hell you been for the past couple days? I've been tryna call you!"

"I'm sorry Daddy! I've been over a trick's house."

She could see Rose losing his temper through the phone.

"Bitch! I don't care who you wit! You better bring that motherfuckin bread!"

Sunshine knew it was gonna be some shit for her disappearing like she did.

"Don't worry Daddy! I'll bring it as soon as I leave!" She lied, stalling for time. She hadn't gotten a dime from Cam'ren. She'd gotten drunk with him and never handled her business like she always did.

She hung up real quick and prayed that no one had told Ross that she was in Cam'ren's room.

Cam'ren came back 20 minutes later with the food in his hands. He walked over to one of his coffee tables after closing his front door.

"Here Baby!" He said while setting her food on the side of the bed.

The tray had hotcakes, pork bacon, and fried eggs. The aroma made Sunshine's mouth water. "Thank you baby!"

Cam'ren smiled at her proudly, "Oh! That ain't it. I got a toothbrush inside of here for you too!"

Sunshine smacked her lips and rolled her eyes, "What you tryna say, my breath stink?"

She reached up to snatch the toothbrush and the sheet fell away from her chest.

Cam'ren got a really good look at her nice perky breasts.

"Oops!" She said while pulling the sheet back up.

Cam'ren laughed, "It ain't like I ain't never seen em before!" He said with a smile.

Sunshine smacked her lips again while rolling her eyes. "Boy you so crazy!"

Cam'ren squatted down and kissed her. When they pulled apart he whispered, "And you are so sexy! You know that?"

Sunshine jumped out of the bed, "Let me go to the bathroom and freshen up!"

Her nice firm ass just bounced in perfect time to her footsteps as Cam'ren watched at attention.

A moment later she came out and sat across from Cam'ren.

"So what's on the agenda for today?" He asked while chewing on a piece of pork bacon.

Sunshine thought for a moment. "I don't know, but I need to get to work. My Boss is on my ass!"

Cam'ren nodded his understanding then inquired, "What type of work do you do?" As he stuck his fork into his hotcakes.

Sunshine tried to be vague. She didn't want him to know what kind of a girl she really was.

"I do a little bit of this and a little bit of that."

"Meaning?" Cam'ren asked.

"I....I."

Her words were cut short from a knock on the door.

Cam'ren got up to answer the door, "Hold that thought. I'll be right back."

Sunshine was relieved and let some much needed air out of her lungs.

Cam'ren was putting her under too much pressure and asking too many questions she didn't want to answer.

When Cam'ren opened the door, there stood a muscular guy with his face all balled up. He looked Cam'ren up and down and then looked past him into the room.

Cam'ren brought his attention back to him. "Can I help you with something brother?"

The dude flexed on Cam'ren then responded, "Yeah! I'm looking for Sunshine."

Sunshine jumped up at the sound of Ross' voice. "I'm here!"

Cam'ren looked back at Sunshine like she was crazy and then turned back to Ross. "Who's this?"

Sunshine broke her neck getting to the door and then chimed in, "This is my brother!

Cam'ren turned to greet the big dude. "What's up homie? I'm her "

He didn't know what he should say. He'd only known Sunshine for a few days.

Sunshine tried to cut the conversation short as she cut her eyes at Cam'ren.

"Is everything alright?" She asked Ross with her face broken up. She was pissed off that Ross had the nerve to come over to Cam'ren's dorm room.

Ross tried to play it off. "Mommy is sick and I need you to come home." He shot back.

Sunshine rolled her eyes and smacked her lips in frustration.

"What's wrong with her?" She asked, trying to be smart.

Ross gave her the grit with his eyes. "That thing!"

His eyes let her know that she'd better bring her ass on or there was gonna be trouble.

She saw the signs and rushed over to the

bed to grab her belongings, then grabbed her jacket off the back of the chair. She rushed to get up out of there.

What none of them noticed was that Nancy hid right down the hallway listening to the whole conversation.

Sunshine stopped at the door, kissed Cam'ren on the cheek, and said, "Alright Baby! I have to go! I'll call you later!" As she stepped out of his room.

Cam'ren watched her roll out and hollered down the hall after her, "I hope your mother gets better!"

He closed the door and went to get ready for his brother's arrival.

As soon as they were out of sight, Ross gripped Sunshine up by the throat.

"Bitch! You better have gotten some chips outta dat square motherfucker! Ain't no free pussy jumpin off here!"

Sunshine cringed as he slammed her up against the hallway's wall pleading, "Come on Daddy! You're making too much noise inside of this building!"

Ross got right up in her face as he continued his gorilla pimpin, "Come on Daddy my ass! You betta get on that stroll and you betta have my paper, fo I stomp a mud hole in dat fat ass o' yours!"

Tears started rollin down Sunshine's face. She was scared he was gonna beat her to death.

"I'll do whatever Daddy! Please let me go so

we can get out of here."

With that, Ross dropped her back down onto her feet and turned to leave.

****

Nancy took in their whole conversation from inside the shower area. With the door cracked she listened until she heard the door slam shut just beneath where she stood listening.

Nancy couldn't wait to get the information she'd heard back to Cam'ren.

When the coast was clear, she shot straight to Cam'ren's door and started knockin like she was tryin to wear a hole in it.

"Hold the hell up!" Cam'ren yelled as he came back to the door to see who it was.

Cam'ren saw who it was and started to slam the door in her face. Nancy put her foot on the door. Seeing that he couldn't slam the door in Nancy's face he looked at her like she was crazy.

"What the fuck do you want Nancy!"

Nancy kept her foot in place so he'd listen to her.

"For starters, I saw your little girlfriend with her pimp!"

Cam'ren didn't know what the hell she was talkin about.

"You don't know shit! That was her brother.

"What do you mean, HER PIMP?!"

Nancy laughed in his face. "Like I said, that

bitch that you falling so hard for is a corner hoe!"

Cam'ren just shook his head.

"What is it Nancy? You like to see me hurting? Is that it?"

He noticed someone coming up the hall behind her. Nancy followed his eyes behind her thinking Sunshine or Ross had come back and was standing behind her.

She had to do a double take to make sure her eyes weren't playing tricks on her. For a minute, Nancy just stood there with her mouth hanging open.

Cam'ron walked up with his partner Smash in tow and just smiled at his brother and Nancy's response when they saw him.

"What the fuck is goin on here?" Nancy asked after getting her voice back.

"Bitch it don't matter if she's a hoe or not. What I do know is that she ain't a bigger hoe than you!"

His remark caught Nancy off guard. Cam'ron and Cam'ren both smiled at each other.

She could see that he intended to play the hell out of her in front of his brother and his homie.

Cam'ron excused himself and stepped between the two of them to give his brother a hug as Nancy and Smash stood watching their exchange.

When they separated, Cam'ron looked back at Nancy with lust in his eyes.

"I see you got a lot of work on your hands."

Cam'ren brushed Nancy off.

"Naw bro, I dismissed this hoe a minute ago. What she needs to do is go out on the stroll and get my money!" Cam'ren yelled in her face.

That really pissed Nancy off.

"Fuck you," she yelled as she turned and stormed her way past Smash and down the hallway.

They watched her leave then Cam'ron turned to his brother. "My little brother by a few minutes is a P.I.M.P. huh?"

Cam'ren tried to play it cool.

"I ain't no P-Love, but I do gets mines!" He lied knowing damn well he was a sucker for love.

Cam'ron motioned Smash over and introduced him.

"This here is my homie Smash. Smash, this here is my twin brother Cam'ren."

Smash couldn't believe the uncanny resemblance they had.

He jumped out of the trance he was in and extended his hand. "What's up my dude?"

"Ain't shit," Cam'ren responded as he returned the handshake.

"Ay yo'! You and your brother sure do look exactly alike. Somebody could get you two mixed up!"

Cam'ren and Cam'ron both looked at each other and responded at the same time.

"We might have to do that one day with some bitches!"

They came into the room and got themselves settled. Cam'ren offered them something to drink, then kicked back to bust up with his brother and Cam'ron's friend.

Cam'ron broke the ice.

"What's up for tonight?"

"Depends on what y'all wanna get into" Cam'ren responded.

Money and bitches!" Smash chimed in while he rubbed his hands together like he was tryna keep them warm.

Cam'ren laughed.

"I can get 'all the bitches. The money is up to you!"

"Don't worry about the money part. I got all the paper we need covered!" Cam'ron interjected, looking over at his partner with a knowing smile.

Cam'ren nodded his understanding.

"We can hit the strip after I get dressed. Where y'all stayin at?"

They'd secured a room at the Motel 6 on their way into town.

Cam'ren just wanted to know since it was obvious there wasn't enough room at his dorm.

"I would've offered y'all a spot here, but you see what I'm workin wit."

With that settled, Cam'ren stepped into the small private bathroom to get dressed. When he came out he had on a pair of light blue denim jeans, a really colorful Polo button up preppy shirt, and some Polo Dock siders.

He looked like a real nerd with the shit he was wearing. Both Cam'ron and Smash bust out laughing in right away.

Cam'ren looked down at his clothes, puzzled.

"What? I have something on my clothes?"

They both stopped laughing and looked at Cam'ren like he was crazy. Cam'ron jumped in.

"Naw Bro! But you ain't goin outwit us lookin like dat der are you? You look like a white boy!"

Cam'ren looked at his clothes again, then back at Cam'ron and his homie Smash.

"You think I look like a white boy?"

"Hell to the yeah!" Smash answered while he turned up his nose at the shit Cam'ren had on.

Cam'ren didn't seem, to agree. He liked the stuff he had on.

"This is what the ladies down here like! Now watch my work tonight!"

He wiped himself down like his hands were rags, then went and checked himself in the mirror like he always did right before going out.

When he was satisfied, they headed out to a club he'd heard about called Club Butterfly on the strip.

They jumped into Cam'ren's car and turned on BG from Cash Money through the system as they pulled out.

After about thirty minutes, they found Club Butterfly and pulled into the parking lot. They all get out of the car and headed inside.

The place was packed. Women of every size,

shape, and nationality worked the room with hardly anything on.

Some women were bent over men's laps doing bank head bounces to the beat while the men put bills into their thong strings.

Most of the women could've been on America's Next Top Model but were shaking their asses for bread instead.

CHAPTER 8

Ross and Sunshine arrived back at the little shabby apartment they'd both been living in for the past two years.

As soon as Ross shut the door he let into Sunshine as he slammed her up against the wall.

"Since you ain't run that money in for the past coupla days, you gonna be workin overtime at the Butterfly!"

He saw the way that Sunshine looked at him. She would've been a "really" attractive woman if she'd have received the proper care. Instead, she'd been dogged out by having to work the streets.

Ross didn't have the luxury of having pitty for her. He had a heroin and crack habit that he had to maintain. That coupled with all the bills they had coming in meant somebody had to be a provider. He didn't have any skills to speak of besides pimpin women.

Sunshine started complaining just to find a way out of working in the club. She hated it! She didn't want to dance for all those dirty men who just felt her up for money.

"I don't have anything to dance in at the club!"

Ross had that covered. "Don't worry, I got

everything you need right here!" He said while pulling a bag from beside the couch.

Ross had one of his best boosting hoes grab some things for her to wear.

His booster made sure that she grabbed the nicest things for Ross' girls to wear at the club. Nice outfits always meant more money.

Sunshine looked at all of the clothes and was impressed at what she saw. She hadn't bathed good in over a week and didn't want to put on the new items without bathing first.

"Let me go soak in the tub before I head out to work?" She asked as she looked at Ross.

She was still sore from all the dick Cam'ren was throwin up in her over the past few days.

Ross let her go and she made her way to the bathroom. "Hoe don't be in there all fuckin day! We have paper to get and we ain't gonna get it while you soakin that ole beat up pussy of yours!" He yelled after her.

Ross started feeling the junky itch as he rubbed his massive biceps. While Sunshine started cleaning up he slid into the kitchen to shoot the last of his dope.

As he sat there nodding, he thought of all the money he needed. The car was about to be repossessed, he was late on the rent, and had just barely been able to pay his booster so Sunshine could have some new clothes to work in.

Sunshine hadn't noticed all the weight that Ross was losing over the past few months.

He was still a big man, it was just that the drugs were starting to read on his body.

While Ross sat in the kitchen nodding, Sunshine soaked her abused body in the bathroom. She thought about Cam'ren. She never met a man who treated her the way that Cam'ren did. Her past few days with him had been unbelievable.

She'd never felt for anyone the way that she'd started feeling about him.

At one time she thought she was in love with Ross. A lot of good that did her. The only thing that he loved was for her to go out there and get his money.

She thought back to the one time he made her have sex with an 89 year old white man while his 20 year old wife fucked her in the ass with a 12 inch dildo.

She had to soak in the tub for a couple of days then too.

The trauma, of all the experiences she'd faced under Ross tyranny had her fucked up, emotionally, physically, and spiritually.

Her love ended for Ross after he'd made her walk the track for three days after what that white couple did to her insides.

She wanted to leave Ross, but she didn't have any place she could go. Now after the stunt he'd pulled with Cam'ren, she knew it was time to leave. She just didn't know if Cam'ren would take her if he knew the truth about her

After a while Ross came out of his nod and

came banging on the door to get her to hurry up.

"Come on woman! I told you we don't have all day!"

Sunshine damn near jumped out of the tub she was so scared. Soap went everywhere as water spilled out of the tub.

"Damn!" She said, sucking her teeth. "I'm coming Ross."

Ross kicked the old wooden door clean off the hinges. In his hands he held two bikini outfits for her to wear.

He looked at the water on the floor then back at Sunshine as she cringed back down into the tub.

"Bitch! I said let's go! It's money to be made and you owe me! We ain't gonna get it with yo' ass laid up in the tub!"

Sunshine hopped up out of the tub with the quickness. She threw a towel down on the floor to soak up the water she splashed, then hurried into the next room to get dressed.

Ross watched every curve of her body as she put on the first outfit. She started oiling her body from head to toe so that her caramel skin would shine in the club's low lighting.

She put on her Diamond Princess perfume, then put on a white see through skirt over top of the outfit she planned on dancing in.

Ross examined her admiringly. "Das what I'm talkin bout! You got a nigga's dick hard and everything."

Sunshine slid into some six inch high red

pumps to finish the ensemble, then she grabbed her duffel bag and was ready to go.

They jumped into Ross' 2XT Escalade truck. He had 24 inch Platinum Bomber rims on it. They pulled out of the parking lot and headed for the Butterfly Club. During the ride over, Sunshine laid back and just listened to Trina's Baddest Chick song.

25 Minutes later they pulled into V.I.P. parking at the back of the club.

Ross got out with Sunshine and banged on the back door while Sunshine waited. A few minutes later, a 300 pound white man with a Mohawk opened the door.

The bouncer and Ross spoke for a moment, then the bouncer looked at Sunshine.

"You are one fine piece of ass girl! Show me what you workin with!"

Sunshine wasn't tryna hear the shit comin out of the white, overweight, wanna be Mystical's mouth.

"Too bad you won't be tastin none of this platinum plus pussy here!" She said as she rubbed her hands down over her coochie while balling up her face.

The bouncer looked at Ross and winked. "I already paid for dat ass tonight!"

Sunshine looked over at Ross who gave her the, "You know the deal" look.

"I know you didn't get no money from this cracker motherfucker to fuck me? Did you?"

Ross just shrugged.

"When you get done dancin, handle that!" He said back to her.

Sunshine gave him the fuck you look while squeezing past the two big men. She made her way back to the dressing room where all of the dancers changed and put on their makeup.

Right then and there Sunshine knew that she was done with Ross. There would be no more hoe strolling for her. The first chance she got, she was out of there. She just had to bide her time.

She wished that she'd never run away at the age of 15. She was almost 25 years old and couldn't believe that she'd been on the streets for nearly ten years.

She thought she was getting her cherry popped by the man of her dreams when she first met Ross.

Now she didn't know what she was supposed to do. She would've liked to have worked in an office, or something else like most normal people, but those dreams were gone since she could hardly read.

All she knew was the streets and what Ross had taught her. He'd taught her the rules of the game in the beginning and led her to believe that they were partners. Now she knew better. That was just part of the game.

Maybe if she'd have stayed in school she wouldn't have been in the predicament that she was now.

A thick and well-tanned white girl came over to chat for a few. Kimberly was about 5'9" with the body of a black woman.

Kimberly was Marty the Club owner's best dancer. Marty was also her sugar daddy.

Kimberly did whatever she wanted in the club since she brought in the most money and was fucking Marty.

Sunshine could tell that Kimberly had an attitude by the way she rolled up.

"Where you been at Sunshine? You think you can just stroll up in here and shake yo fat ass in here whenever you want?"

Sunshine just ignored her since she wasn't her boss. When Kimberly got no response, she stormed out of the room to take the stage.
A new girl walked up to Sunshine and introduced herself.

"Don't worry about that bitch, she's just a hater. By the way, my name is Amber," she said while extending her hand.

Sunshine took her hand and introduced herself. For some reason Sunshine got a good vibe from Amber.

As it turns out, Amber was a runaway just like Sunshine. She started working in clubs at the age of 14 by lying about her age to the different club owners.

She'd been at it for four years now and had her own apartment as a result of it.

She had men coming and going from her place at all hours of the night, but she paid her bills, and kept all of her money.

She broke all of that down for Sunshine in

less than twenty minutes as Sunshine got ready for her set.

At least she has her own place, Sunshine thought to herself. Amber had started out like Sunshine did, with a pimp. When she realized she could make more money by herself, she left him. Now she was getting all of the benefits for what she was forced to do and it encouraged Sunshine.

She looked at Amber and realized that she was really just a black girl trapped in a white girl's body. She supposed that that was why all the black guys liked her.

On a slow night, she easily raked in a grand or more.

On a Friday or Saturday, she generally made three grand easily.

Since it was a Friday, Sunshine could only imagine how much money the white girl was gonna make at Club Butterfly between dancing and sellin pussy.

Sunshine removed her blond, purple, and red wigs trying to decide on which one to wear so she could up her competitiveness at getting some of the money that was out there.

"I like the blonde one!" Amber said while looking over Sunshine's voluptuous body in the full length mirror.

Sunshine knew the look that Amber was giving her. Most of the women that danced were bi-sexual.

Sunshine settled on the blonde wig too as

she tied her hair down with a stocking cap and then slid the wig on over it.

She checked herself once more, then made her way to the stage.

"Knock em' dead girl!" Amber hollered after her while slapping her on the ass.

"Shake What Yo' Momma Gave You" was playing when Sunshine walked onto the stage. She worked the pole like a skilled gymnast. The men went crazy throwing money at her.

Kimberly stood on the side of the stage hating at all the attention that Sunshine was getting.

Sunshine turned her back to the audience while bending over, then she dropped low before shaking her ass from the split position.

Sunshine tried not to focus too much on the audience. She briefly spotted Ross watching her over at the bar as she bent over to grab her ankles.

As she stepped to hit another pole move, she could've sworn she saw someone that looked just like Cam'ren in the crowd of onlookers.

She hurried up and gathered her money and shot straight off the stage. She couldn't be sure if it was him, but she definitely didn't want him seeing her like that if it was. She ducked into the dressing room and prayed to God it wasn't him.

CHAPTER 9

Pam, sat staring out of the bay window of her and Cam'ron's home. The place was beautiful.

She had everything that a woman could want in terms of worldly possesions.

What she didn't have was someone who really loved her.

She sat in her huge house rubbing her stomach and wondering whose child she carried. She knew that keeping her child might mean "death for her." Especially if it wasn't Cam'ron's child.

She called Troy. "Yo!"

"What up Ma?" Troy answered with an attitude. They'd been arguing with each other for the past few weeks and Pam could see that he still wasn't over it.

Pam sucked her lips away from the phone then tried to calm down. "I need you to come over so I can talk to you."

She could just imagine Troy's face ballin up on the other end of the line.

She would've been wrong....

Troy was on the other end of the line hittin Summer from the back! He ain't have time ta talk. He was about to nut in some good pussy, "BAREBACK"!

"Yo!" — "Oooh shit dis pussy is good," he thought as he paused in his answer— "Can I call you back LATER!"

Pam could tell Troy didn't wanna to talk to her. "Troy! I need you to come by the house when you get done. We need to talk!"

Troy twisted his lips and pumped faster after slappin Summer on the ass.

"I'll be over there. I gotta go!"

He hung up the phone so he could focus on what he was doin. (Fuckin his father's girl Summer)

Troy dropped the phone by the side of the bed for a minute as he pulled out.

That Summer was one of his father's women didn't matter to Troy.

Pussy was pussy and Troy didn't have no rules when it came to where he got it from. Especially if it was some good pussy!

Summer crawled across the bed and threw her legs up in an open split like the professional stripper that she was. She stuck her fingers inside of herself to wet them, then started rubbin her swollen clit to tease Troy.

Summer was a freak!

Troy slid up and started helpin her with his lips as Summer moaned while grinding her insides in his face.

Troy licked up and down her pink lips and sucked her clit like he was suckin on grapes. He worked his tongue deep up inside of Summer's hot box until she came hard on his face.

As she lay shivering from the afterglow, Troy worked his way up her stomach till he was positioned between her legs.

She pulled them back to the head board to welcome him, while Troy took her to Bed Rock.

Pop-pop-pop-pop-pop!

Like a jack hammer, Troy started wearin the ass out until he came all on her stomach.

He was hittin it raw, but he ain't want no more babies.

He'd been seeing Summer at the same time that he was seeing Pam and hadn't been having protected sex with either one of them.

When he was done, he took a quick shower while Summer lay in his father's bed.

When he came out 30 minutes later, he smacked Summer on the ass and left a message for his father.

"Tell Pops I stopped by and I'ma handle dat business in a minute."

Summer giggled, rolled over, and went to sleep.

****

Troy headed over to Cam'ron's house. When he got there, Pam was waiting with the mad face for him.

"What, up Ma? What you wanna see me for?"

Pam was tired of his attitude so she got right to the point. "I need you to take me to the all night clinic in Sumter!"

Troy looked at her like he couldn't understand what she was saying.

"What kinda clinic is open this time of night?" He asked, trying to figure out what she was ready to get into.

"I need to see the doctor about something! Just come on so you can take me!"

Pam could've taken herself, but if she really needed an abortion, she knew she'd need someone to take her home afterwards.

Troy didn't ask any more questions. Troy knew he was on some nut shit fuckin with Cam'ron's woman after all that they'd been through.

They'd started rollin together before Pam, Shamrock, or Smash had ever even come into the picture.

Troy was just a dirty nigga. He was just like his father. He ain't have no loyalty to anyone but himself.

For him, it wasn't about nothin to fuck your homies girl.

Shit! He was fuckin his father's woman!

He walked with Pam back out the house, jumped in his Smoke Gray Mustang, and pulled out of the driveway blasting the Carter One through his system.

Pam just sat there stewing the whole way to the highway. She was mad that Troy was actin like he really didn't give a fuck about her, so she said, "Fuck it!", and told him why she needed to see the doctor.

Pam hit the mute button on Troy's system. "Troy, I'm pregnant!"

He was quiet for a minute. His face didn't give away any of his feelings.

"So what are we going to do about the baby?" He asked as he kept his eyes on the road.

Pam didn't know how to take his response at all!

"What do you mean?"

Troy looked at her sideways with a blank expression.

"Are you going to kill my baby?"

Pam couldn't believe this fool.

"You don't even know if in fact this baby is even yo's!"

"I know in my heart that the baby you carrying is mines!" He said as he tightened his jawline.

"What? You psychic now?" Pam asked with her eyes wide.

"I just told you that I can feel it in my heart. Plus we can take a paternity test and if it turns out to be mines then we'll keep it!"

"So what if it doesn't turn out to be yours?"

"Well if it ain't mine, then you can get rid of it!"

He didn't care if the baby was Cam'ron's baby he was killing, as long as it wasn't his.

"Hell no! If I know the paternity and it's his, then I wouldn't kill it! He's my future husband!"

She shot back with a serious look.

"So yo' ass is telling me that if it's my baby, your going to kill it, but if it's that nigga's, you keepin it?"

Pam nodded with the, Duuuuuuh expression.

"Yes that's what I'm saying. I thought you were his friend?"

Pam got a nasty vibe from Troy when she said that. The way he looked and the way he was actin wasn't right. Just mentioning Cam'ron around him made him mad and she could see it on his face.

"He is, but your going to kill my seed. Dat nigger ain't better than me, nor is his seed! Fuck dat!"

"I think we need to stop seeing each other. You on some other shit!" Pam said.

So now you don't wanna fuck wit a nigga like dat no mo'?"

Troy pulled up in front of the clinic and grabbed Pam by her clothes. Pam had never seen this side of Troy. He had rage in his eyes. She tried not to look at those eyes for fear that she'd get weak.

"Get off me!" She screamed as tears of love and hate rolled down her face.

Pam loved Troy. In another situation they would've probably stayed together. Troy put in work in the bedroom, but he already had a woman.

At the same time, Troy really loved Pam. What was supposed to be a one night stand to get back at Cam'ron for his having cheated on her, turned into their cheating so many times they couldn't count.

Their sexing turned into months, then years. Now Troy was in love with Pam.

That Troy already had someone in his life didn't matter to him. He wanted Pam too.

"All you gotta do is find out whose baby it is! We can work out the rest from there!"

What he didn't say was that he didn't believe Cam'ron was going to be around much longer anyway!

Pam agreed to get a paternity test just to calm Troy down. In her mind, she had to do what she had to do. If she got the abortion, he couldn't say anything since what would be done would be done. It was her decision.

"Alright I'll do the test!" She lied.

Troy seemed relieved. He calmed down and started climbing out of the car.

Pam stepped out and followed behind him. They both walked through the two sliding glass doors to the male nurse sitting behind an island desk.

"Can I help you?" He asked in a gay nasal tone. Pam just shook her head. It was sad for a gay nigga to be so fine.

When she saw how the punk was all up on Troy, she intercepted that shit.

"Yes! I have an appointment under da name Pamela Good!" She said while standing there with her arms folded over her hips.

"The faggot looked down and started to check his computer as they waited.

"Oh, I see your name. The doctor has been waiting on you.

"You can head back into room three."

Pam took a final look back at Troy as he took a seat, then took the hallway leading to the abortion of her child.

She knocked on door number three and found her doctor waiting on her.

"Hi, I'm Mrs. Wilson," she announced as Pam stepped into the room.

"How are you feeling today?"

"I'm not feeling too good about what I might need done." Pam said as she sat down.

The doctor tried to comfort her.

"Well, abortion is never an easy choice. Your aware that the test for whether you were pregnant came back positive. Now you may choose to keep the child or terminate the pregnancy. That choice is yours.

"Either way, you should also get tested for any sexually transmitted diseases. That way if you do decide to keep the child you'll know that the pregnancy will be safe.

"If you decide to terminate the pregnancy, you should consider some type of birth control during intercourse to avoid this problem in the future. Birth control pills will not keep you from contracting HIV, AIDS, or any other sexually transmitted diseases. So, we suggest that in the future you use a condom when having sex.

"Now if you'll let me, I'd like to draw some blood and send it for testing. While I'm doing that, you can decide if you also want to terminate the pregnancy."

Pam sat numbly as the woman told her all of this. She hadn't had protected sex with Troy, and she doubted that he protected himself when he was with his own woman.

Cam'ron had already given her an STD while he was cheating. So she worried that he could have given her something again as well.

The realization of all these poor decisions amounted to her having to abort a child. The sad thing was that even she didn't know which one was her baby's father.

That coupled with the fact that if it wasn't Cam'ron's meant she might get killed if he found out was enough for her to make up her mind regarding what had to be done.

A few hours later, Pam woke up with cotton ball mouth.

"Is it over?" Pam asked with a slur in her voice.

"Yes, it's over. Do you have someone to drive you home?" Asked Dr. Wilson.

"Yes, I think he's still out there waiting."

"Alright, you'll experience some bleeding that may last for a few days. If it gets heavy, you are to go to the hospital.

"Here are some pills for the pain. Take them three times a day for a week. We'll let you know the results of your blood work when it comes. If you have any questions or you need someone to talk to, feel free to use the 1-800 number on this card."

With that, Pam got up and walked back down the hall. When Pam walked out, Troy got up from where he was sitting.

"So are they gonna do the test?" He asked while holding Pam up.

Pam couldn't even look at Troy. Her insides hurt and she was still light headed from the anesthesia.

"There ain't gonna be no tests. I had the pregnancy terminated!" Pam said in a drunkin slur.

"What! You killed my baby?!? I thought you were going to wait until after the test!"

Hurt was written all over Troy's face. Pam looked at him with tears in her eyes.

"I didn't want to go through all of that, so I did what I thought was the right decision."

Pam started pulling Troy toward the exit. She didn't want the people inside of the clinic all up in her business.

Troy pulled back when they got outside.

"Naw yo', you ain't gettin in "my" car! Yo' ass can catch a cab or walk yo' stinkin ass home! That was some foul shit you pulled!"

Pam felt like somebody had slapped her senseless. She couldn't believe Troy was pulling his shit.

"Nigga, what yo' ass mean I have to catch a cab? You brought me here and you takin me home!"

Troy flagged her and started gettin in the car.

"Like I said trick. Catch a motherfuckin cab or walk yo' ass home!"

Pam stepped on his heels not caring who heard her now.

"Fuck yo' ass motherfucker! Das why I got the abortion! Yeah Motherfuckah! It was yo' baby! You think I wanna have a baby by yo' nothin ass?"

Troy wanted to climb out of his car and kill Pam, on the spot. He almost slapped the shit of her right then and there, but she kept goin.

"Yeah! The dick was good, but it's over! I'm stayin with Cam'ron!"

Troy just flagged her. In his mind, Cam'ron wasn't gonna be around for long. He had something for all that shit.....

It was only a matter of time.

CHAPTER 10

Cam'ren, Cam'ron and Smash sat comfortably in the V.I.P. section of Club Butterfly. They all were looking around at the thick dancers as the strobe lights of the club hit ass cheeks and titties in multiple colors.

Cam'ron and Smash both knew they had to get some pussy before the night was over.

The club had every flavor that a man could ask for. Black, Asian, Spanish, or white, the Butterfly Club had whatever you liked.

In the center of the club stood a stage with varying performers rotating with the change of songs. Featured dancers worked the pole while men sat at the stage's edge and made it rain for their favorite dancers.

As "Shake What Your Mamma Gave You" started pumping through the club's speakers, a chick with a coke bottle body came out in a blond wig. The men cheered as she started droppin it like it was hot to the beat. There were so many men at the base of the stage that it was hard to see the featured dancer.

Cam'ren looked over and enjoyed the quick glimpse he had of the newest dancer's body. The shape of her body reminded him of Sunshine's.

She slid back down the pole and out of view while the familiarity of the way she looked seemed to bother Cam'ren. The chick looked a lot like Sunshine!

Before he could get a better look at the dancer's face, she was leaving the stage for the next dancer.

"Yo', I could'a sworn that I saw my chick!" Stated Cam'ren over the loud music.

Smash looked over to see a fat ass and blond wig steppin off the stage.

"Yo' my dude, if that was yo' chick, she one bad Mamma Jamma!" Smash responded in a tipsy tone.

"I'm not sayin it was her, but it damn sure looked like her from the back!" Stated Cam'ren while rubbing his little chin hairs and thinking about the good time he and Summer had shared in bed.

"If she got an ass like the chick that just got finished dancin, all I wanna know is if she got some girlfriends!" Smash replied with raised eye brows.

Cam'ren didn't really know anything about Summer so he told the truth. "I don't know if she got any girlfriends. I haven't known her that long."

Cam'ron looked at his brother with a lot of doubt. He'd seen Nancy, and if his other friend was half as fine as her, he might be able to hook them up.

"Yeah right! You prob'ly tryna keep all the pussy fo' yo'self. I know she has to have a few girlfriends!" Stated Cam'ron.

With that, Smash pulled out a Dutch Master filled with Purple Haze.

"You smoke?" He asked Cam'ren.

"Naw!"

"Damn, you don't smoke? Yo' ass is really lame!" Stated Cam'ron while looking over at his brother.

Cam'ren could see that his brother really didn't understand what he aspired to become. He tried to explain it to him. "I'm not try'na fuck up what I'm try'na do. I've worked real hard for the past few years and I'm almost there."

Cam'ron just listened to his brother. This was the first time they'd had to talk about what Cam'ren's future plans were and why he was going to school.

"So what are you goin to school for?"

"I'm about to take the bar exam after Home Coming week is over."

"Oh shit! I My brother is try'na be a lawyer!" Cam'ron announced proudly as he jumped out of his chair and hugged his brother.

Smash sat watching the women walk by while he nursed his drink. He smiled his own approval. Lawyers made money and to have one in the family could be helpful to Cam'ron's business.

When Cam'ron let go of a blushing Cam'ren, he just shrugged his shoulders.

"I just hope I pass it man. This shit is hard and requires a lot of studying. I'm gonna have to put in some studying time while y'all are here.

You don't mind do you?"

Cam'ron punched his brother on the shoulder, "Naw Bro, you do what you gotta do. We'll be alright! I think this shit calls for a celebration. Drinks on me!"

Smash pulled out a wad of cash that had every stripper's radar go off. They'd been playing it cool up in V.I.P. and it was time to get the party started! "I got the drinks. What y'all want?"

"I want that Patrone Baby! Bring the whole bottle! What you want bro?"

Cam'ren was already a little tipsy from the contact he was catchin off of Smash's Dutch. The smoke was makin him feel real good, but he still had to study in the morning. He wanted to keep a clear head.

"Just give me a beer yo', I'll be alright with that."

"Awww hell naw!" Smash shot back!

"Dis here is a party dawg. We celebratin a family reunion. You can't do that with no beer! We gotta loosen you up some!"

Just as he said this, a fly assed Amber came by catching all their attention.

Smash was on it right away as he held a stack of 100 dollar bills in his hand the size of a head of cabbage. "Ay yo' I like dat der' Shawty! Can we get a dance?"

Amber had all eyes on that money, "I can get a few friends and we can go to the Champagne Room!"

She signaled to two other girls after looking

around the room and not seeing Sunshine, the person she was looking for.

The women flocked around the men like crazy as the other men looked on with hate in their eyes.

They grabbed their drinks and took the party to the back room. There was a trail of ass and tits everywhere as all the women tried to shake their asses extra hard competing for the three men's attention.

Ross watched all of this from the bar. He recognized Cam'ren as being the cat that Sunshine had disappeared with and wondered if she hadn't been lying to him about getting bread from the dude. He had another dude with him that was obviously his twin brother. They looked exactly alike, and he wondered who the other cat smokin the Dutch was who kept spending all the money.

He got up to find Sunshine and put her ass on the paper her trick was spending. She shoulda had dibs on that shit since she'd been fuckin him for three days and he intended to make sure she got it.

When he got to the back he found Sunshine arguing with her clothes on. Lucky for Ross, the bouncer with the mohawk had her caught tryna leave.

As he rolled up, the big dude noticed him and turned to address his business to him.

"What type a shit is this bitch tryna pull Ross? I paid for a shot of that pussy and I catch this bitch sneakin out the back door?"

Ross drew back without saying a word and hit Sunshine with a body shot that made her fold up like a collapsible chair.

"Bitch! Didn't I tell you to get ya' funky ass up on the stage and get money? What kinda games you playin wit me, tryna leave and shit! You gon' make me kill you?"

Sunshine couldn't talk. Ross had knocked all the air out of her and when she did try to inhale, her ribs screamed at her in rebellion.

When she didn't answer, Ross grabbed her by the back of her neck and pulled her back up to a standing position while he got up in her face with his fouled breath.

"You gon' handle dat business wit dis man like I told you to, and den you gon' carry yo' funky ass back out onto dat floor and get that money from yo' boyfriend and his friends! Unda' stand me ho'?"

Sunshine nodded as he let her go. She looked over at the fat cracker who's mouth seemed to be watering in anticipation of having his way with her. She cringed at the thought as Ross stepped off and left her with the trick.

The bouncer grabbed Sunshine by the arm and dragged her to the parking lot where he had his car. He threw her into the passenger seat, then walked around and got inside on the driver's side.

As soon as the big man squeezed beneath the steering wheel he started unzipping his pants and breathing real heavy as he told Summer to suck his dick first.

Sunshine could barely see anything in his lap over the pink folds of fat and hairy belly that brushed up against the steering wheel. There wasn't even room for her to get to what he had under all the folds of fat.

The bouncer didn't seem to realize this and began pushing her head between his funky stomach and the steering wheel.

As he did this, Sunshine tried to brace herself on the seat and nearly fell face first as he forced her head down. She put her hand down for purchase and touched the floorboard of the car. Her hand hit on a long screw driver and she instinctively wrapped her hands around it. The man kept forcing her head up against his stomach and the steering wheel hurting her ribs even more as she bent.

She screamed, "Wait! Let me get mo comf-ta-bul!"

The man stopped pushing and as Sunshine came up, she planted the screw driver dead in the fat motherfuckers right eye. The fat honky screamed like a little bitch as she kept digging and digging till she hit the back of his fuckin skull.

When he was done shakin, Summer was covered in blood. She reached over and cracked the driver's side door, then leaned up against the passenger's side door with both of her feet on the fat bouncer's arm and stomach.

She kicked with all her might until the bouncer hit the asphalt, then shut the door and pulled off. She didn't know what she was gonna do. She couldn't go back to the club and she knew Ross was gonna kill her the first chance that he got.

She couldn't go to Cam'ren's place since Ross knew where he lived. She thought about the white chick Amber and after remembering where she'd mentioned she lived, decided she'd see if she could help her. But first she had to get some of her clothes and get cleaned up.

****

Amber forgot all about Sunshine as she partied with Cam'ron, Cam'ren and Smash. She was in the presence of ballers from out of town, and just knew she'd be able to go shopping "and" pay the rent with the money these dudes were spending.

She decided to invite the men back to her place so that they could continue the party in private. Cam'ron was on it and just wanted to ditch his brother and Smash. They had to come up with their own pussy. There was enough to go around.

They exited the club and all got into their cars as they took the party to Amber's house. The drive over looked like a Presidential Motorcade as they blasted "Go Dee-Jay" by Lil Wayne on the ride over.

When they parked, Cam'ron could see that Cam'ren wasn't faded like everyone else. He slid him off to the side to have a talk with him before they finished the celebration.

"What's up Bro? Everything aiight?"

Cam'ren seemed distracted.

"Naw man, I'm good. I just got a lot of studying I gotta do tomorrow."

Cam'ron looked at Cam'ren with a look on his face like he'd just sucked on a lemon.

"Man, what the hell is wrong wit you. We tryna celebrate tonight. That shit can't be that important. Why the hell you wanna be a lawyer anyway?"

Cam'ren looked at his brother trying to find the words to make him understand where he was coming from. "

Man, ever since that shit happened to Daddy, that's what I've wanted to do so that no one else's family has to go through that.

Now I've got a chance to be a Prosecutor & punish people for that kinda shit. I also applied to the F.B.I. and I'm waiting to see if they'll accept me. I just ain't heard back yet."

Cam'ron looked at his brother like he was crazy! In his mind he couldn't imagine why his brother would want to be a cop and let him know it.

"Man, you wanna be an F.B.I. agent? Why the hell you like dat cop shit so much?"

"Because I could look into Pop's murder man. I might be able to find the two bitches that killed him. Do you know how many nightmares I had after that?"

Cam'ron grabbed his brother and looked him in his eyes with his hands on each of his shoulders, so he'd pay attention to him. It was like he was looking at a mirror image of himself, but in another universe where he was a law abiding citizen and not a drug king pin.

"Where I come from we handle our own business in the streets. We don't go tellin, and we don't involve no police. Ya heard me?"

Cam'ren could see that his brother wasn't getting it. "I'm not like you Cam'ron. I ain't from the streets!"

Just then, Smash walked up with a bottle of Crystal in his hands and two chicks hangin on his hips.

"What up my dudes? Why y'all look so down? I thought we was havin a party!" He said with a fresh Dutch of Purple hangin off his lips. Cam'ron and Cam'ren both looked at him.

"We jus discussin fam'ly business my dude" Cam'ron responded as he cut his eyes back at his brother.

"I thought I was fam'ly too!" Smash said like his feelings had been hurt.

"You are, but this is some personal shit."

That ended the conversation between Cam'ron and Cam'ren.

Cam'ron grabbed the bottle from Smash and went looking for Amber while one of the girls on Smash's hip started eying Cam'ren.

She slid up beside him and put her arm in his as she touched his cheek with her hand.

"Damn you fine! Let's have some fun!"

Smash gave Cam'ren the flat tire, then chimed in.

"My dude here is square. He can't hang!"

Cam'ren felt that Smash was challenging his manhood and wanted to prove himself after the conversation that he and his brother had just had.

"I can party you under the table dawg! I ain't dat square! I'm from the Dirty, Ya' heard!"

"Bet a stack on it then playah!"

Cam'ron hollered back, "Bet dat! I got my brother's back!" Then smiled at him.

They moved to the small bar that Amber had in her living room and started setting up shots of Patrone. Within minutes everybody was cheering them on as they downed shot after shot until somebody quit, passed out, or threw up.

Smash was barely hangin onto the table when it was all said and done. He'd already had a few drinks at the club and the shit started catchin up to him.

Cam'ren was feelin it too after about the eighth drink. He was about ready to buckle when Smash fell off the bar stool as everybody started laughing.

The chick next to Cam'ren led him off the bar stool and up the steps to the bathroom. She started kissing on him and rubbing his cheat while she unzipped his pants.

Cam'ren's head kept spinning and within a few minutes found himself sliding down the bathroom wall with the chick eatin his gun up as he passed out.

Downstairs, Cam'ron handed over a few stacks to Amber back in the kitchen to take care of the party. As they sat and talked for a few minutes, he could hear Smash in the other room makin it rain as the women surrounded him.

Somebody came in the front door and one of Amber's friends came to let her know somebody was looking for her.

She excused herself as Cam'ron waited. When she came back she had a fine assed chick in a blond wig with her. Cam'ren whistled, "Damn Shawty, you got some fine assed friends."

The chick in the blond wig looked petrified and stepped over to him like she knew Cam'ron. "What are you doin here?"

Cam'ron was kinda put off by the way the chick was up on him like she knew him and so was Amber.

"Yo' shawty, I know you?" He asked as he started laughing.

The blonde chick looked at Amber sideways, then back at Cam'ron.

"Cam'ren, now you don't know me no more?"

Right then it clicked. This was the girl his brother thought he'd seen dancing up on the stage. The one he told him he hadn't known that long.

He looked her up and down and immediately got aroused. You could see Sunshine's ass from the front it was so fat. She looked a little scruffy in the stuff she had on. Plus she looked a little scared for some reason.

"Yeah baby! I know you! I was just teasin you! Come'eer and give me some love. You know you my Boo!"

Sunshine looked at him suspiciously. She'd never heard Cam'ren talk the way he was. She supposed it was because of the drinks and the party atmosphere, so she let it go.

****

Sunshine turned to Amber, "Can I see you for a minute Amber? I need to talk to you."

They both stepped out of the kitchen while Cam'ron enjoyed the back shot on Sunshine when she stepped out. He had to hit that. The excitement of being able to hit a switch on his brother's girl excited him. He developed a plan as they talked.

When they came back, Cam'ron sat Sunshine on his lap and started pouring her drinks. She seemed real nervous, so Cam'ron used the excuse of getting her to relax to give her more and more drinks until she was faded.

When he was certain that she was feeling the atmosphere, he whispered in her ears, "Let's go somewhere where we can be alone Baby. I've missed you!" He stuck his tongue in her ear then started planting kisses on her neck that got her really aroused.

"Das my spot right der" She cooed as she started grinding her firm ass on Cam'ron's lap.

Before things got too heated, he called out to Amber. She came back to see what he wanted with one of Smash's Dutches, and a tall drink like she was really enjoying herself.

"What up my dude?" She said, impersonating Smash's signature saying.

"We gonna go to the hotel for a minute. Hold my people down until I get back. I got you on a little somethin extra when I come ta pick up my squad."

Amber had already been given $5,000 for the party expenses and couldn't wait to see how much more she'd make.

"I got you. Y'all have a good time. Bye Sunshine!" She chimed as she worked her way back to the party.

****

Cam'ron went up and got his brother's keys while he was knocked out with the stripper in one of Amber's spare rooms. He shook his head in disgust at the sorry state of his brother. As he closed the door and turned off the lights he thought to himself.

"I'ma have to show dis nigga how we do!"

With that, he stepped to the Palmer's Hotel that he and Smash had been staying at. He stepped past the clerk with Sunshine right beside him on wobbly legs. He got her into the room and it was on and poppin!

Within minutes he had Sunshine's see through dress hiked up her back and was wearin the ass out!

"On my God Cam'ren, right there, das my spot!" Sunshine yelled as Cam'ron went deeper, and deeper, drilling into her uterus.

Cam'ron couldn't believe how good the pussy was. She was throwin the ass back at him like a pro, and just before he came, he pulled out to yank the condom off. He shot stream after stream of hot cum all along her back, then rubbed his throbbing penis between her ass cheeks in a slow grinding motion.

He hit the pussy a few more times, then checked to see what time it was.

Sunshine lay beside him under the covers just as she had earlier with Cam'ron's brother.

"Sunshine Baby, we gotta go!" He whispered as she started to wake up.

She was still drunk as hell and he wanted her that way.

He got her up and put her dress back on her. He saw her panties laying in a heap on the floor and grabbed them, tucking them quickly into his pocket.

He drove Cam'ren's car back to Amber's house where most of the party goers had either gone home or fallen asleep. He knocked on the door while holding up a drunk and half sleep

Sunshine.

Amber came to the door, butt naked, and had it not been for all the work Cam'ron had just put in, he would've been tempted to go a few more rounds. There just wasn't time for that.

They stepped in and Cam'ron put Sunshine down on the couch for a minute while he motioned for Amber to follow him into the kitchen.

"Listen Shawty, here's another five stacks for the accommodations. Look out for baby girl in there till we can get back at ya, ya heard."

"Amber didn't ask any questions. Her eyes followed the stacks of green out of Cam'ron's pocket and into her hands. When he counted out the $5,000.00, she sashayed her ass up outta the kitchen and dragged Sunshine's ass up to her room.

Cam'ron woke Smash up on the couch with two butt naked strippers draped all over him and a half smoked Dutch hangin off his lips, and carried him to the car.

Cam'ron came back into the house and went up to get his brother from up underneath the snoring stripper he'd left him with in Amber's spare room. Before he left, Amber came out of the bedroom to wave goodbye.

Cam'ron warned her, "You don't know nothin about no twin. Remember that!" He whispered as he made his way with his brother down the steps.

It finally dawned on Amber why he'd said

that while she was countin her $10,000.00. Cam'ron had just fucked his brother's girl and didn't want Sunshine to know it was really him that did it. It was some foul shit, but she didn't care. She'd just met Sunshine, and if it was profitable, she had no problem keepin her mouth shut since a fuck was a fuck in her mind.

Cam'ron got Smash and Cam'ren back to Cam'ren's dorm room. By the time they got there, the two of them were looking none the worst for wear as they sipped on cups of coffee Cam'ron stopped to get along the way.

Cam'ren and Smash both had the hangover look as they got settled back in Cam'ren's room.

"So what's up for today my dude?" Smash asked Cam'ron as he popped a couple of Tylenol and took a sip of his coffee.

"I don't know yet. I wanted to check with Cam'ren's schedule before I made up my mind.

Cam'ren looked exhausted.

"I gotta go over to the Library for a few hours to get some things together for my exams next week. When I'm finished that, I'll come back and get some sleep, and then we can figure things out from there. If you two want, you can stay here and wait for me, then I'll drive you over to the hotel."

Smash had the, "Say no more," look on his face. He kicked his shoes off and balled straight up on the couch with his coat over his head. Cam'ron got comfortable on his brother's bed.

Cam'ren gathered his things to head over to

the library. Before he left, he took a final swig of the cold coffee to give him energy, then headed out the door.

Cam'ren laid back catching zees for about 45 minutes with Smash snoring on the couch when he heard a knock at the door. He got up and tried to answer the door quietly so he wouldn't wake up Smash on the couch. When he opened the door, Nancy was standing there to greet him.

"I was hoping you were home Cam'ren. We need to have a serious talk!"

Cam'ron tried to shush her and stepped out while closing the door behind him.

"What you wanna talk to me about girl? I thought you was dismissed?"

Nancy tried to look past him as he slid out of the room.

"What, you got that hoe up in your room again? I told you that bitch is a whore, so why you still messin with her when you got all this?"

She said as she held open her trench coat.

Nancy was butter ball naked! Cam'ron couldn't believe his luck! He had a chance to pull a switch two times in one day.

"Naw! It ain't like dat Ma! I got my partnah, I mean my brother's friend staying over and he's sleepin."

Nancy looked at him suspiciously as Cam'ron looked her up and down. Something didn't quite seem right, to her, but she didn't care. She was horny, and addicted to sex. She needed her fix!

"Then why can't I come in and see?" She said as she pulled her jacket closed.

Cam'ron put his finger up to his lips to give her the be quiet while signal, then opened the door.

Smash was laid out on the couch snoring like a banshee when she stepped in.

As she turned thinking that Cam'ren/Cam'ron was going to tell her to leave now, she was taken off guard when he walked up and started kissing her.

Nancy leaned into him, rubbing under his shirt as she raked her nails across his chest like a cat.

Cam'ren/Cam'ron reached down and grabbed two hands full of ass as he picked her up off her feet and started grinding on her in his boxers and a tee shirt.

Nancy moaned and started reaching in his shorts to guide him into her soaking wet insides, while wrapping her legs around his waist in one motion.

Cam'ron carried her over to the bed, put her down, and pulled open her coat. He paused to see if Smash had heard them. He saw no movement, so he pulled down his boxers and slid up in Nancy's tight wet pussy.

She moaned and Cam'ron had to cover her mouth.

"Ooh Cam'ren! I missed you so much baby! You know how much I need you inside me!"

Cam'ron almost laughed in the bitch's face.

He tried to cover her mouth, so she wouldn't wake up Smash as he plowed into the pussy with her legs up, and ass hangin off the bed while he stood on both his feet.

Nancy enjoyed it as her eyes rolled back into her head and she started clawing for something to hold onto.

Cam'ron missed a stroke as he saw movement beside him. He looked over and smiled at Smash with the, "Ain't no fun if the homies can't get none," look on his face.

He started deep stroking Nancy and uncovered her mouth. She held her mouth open wide in ecstasy from how he was hittin her G-spot, and almost choked when Smash stuck his dick in her mouth.

At first she had a shocked expression on her face. Cam'ron popped the pussy harder so she'd open her mouth up wider, and when she did, Smash slid right down her throat with 3 inches of hard Down South Dick.

She had no choice but to take it. She started suckin him off after she saw who she thought was Cam'ren didn't mind. Now she knew who he really was. It was Cam'ron, his twin brother, and she liked it!

She fucked and sucked both of them for an hour, and after that, Cam'ron told the bitch to roll. She left without any arguments since she got what she came for and more.

As Cam'ron and Smash sat back laughin at

Nancy, a 1½ later, somebody else knocked on the door.

Cam'ron thought maybe Nancy had come back for seconds and was surprised when he saw a big muscle bound Ross on the other side of the door.

"What up partner? Can I help you?" He asked as he looked Ross up and down.

"Is Sunshine here?" Ross growled. He ain't have time for conversation.

"I don't know nobody by dat name partner!" Cam'ron said and started to close the door.

Ross pushed the door back and said, "Naw Partner, watch yo' fuckin mouth and open up! I wanna see for myself!" Then he pushed Cam'ron out of the way.

Cam'ron caught him with a two piece combination to the body and as they started tussling, the click of a hammer by Ross's ear took the fight out of him. Smash had a Desert Eagle pointed to his head.

Ross stepped back with his hands up as Cam'ron gathered himself.

"My fault man! I thought my ho was hidin in there! I musta got the wrong room!" Ross replied with fear in his eyes.

Smash pulled the Dutch off his lips and looked over to make sure Cam'ron was cool.

"Ain't no Sunshine here my dude! So bounce!"

Ross turned to leave, when he did, Cam'ron kicked him in the ass as he ran down the hall....

CHAPTER 11

Cam'ren had been studying for finals for nearly two hours. He tried to focus, but found himself nodding off every few pages as he tried to make notes. He just couldn't stay awake. He looked at his watch and decided that he couldn't get anything done in the state he was in, so he decided to call it a wrap.

As he walked back across campus, everyone was in a good mood. The homecoming weekend was in full swing. Most of the people were getting ready for the Jay-Z concert that was scheduled for that night. After that, it was game time, the final football game of the season. Howard had a tough game ahead of them, but were expected to win.

He decided to call Sunshine on the cell phone to see how she was doing. Sunshine picked up after 8 or nine rings and sounded about as bad as he felt.

"Hello?"

"Hey Sunshine, how you doin?" Cam'ren asked, not trying to sound too wore out over the phone.

"I'm fine, I just had a rough night. What are you doin up so early?"

"I just got back from studying and I'm on

my way to get with my brother. I'll probably take him to the concert tonight."

Sunshine really missed Cam'ren. She also had to work out where she was going to stay. If anybody connected her to the fat bouncer's murder, they'd probably try to give her the death penalty. Plus she had to deal with how she was going to get away from Ross's evil ass. She just didn't want Cam'ren to know all that.

"Well, I hope you have a nice time. Tell your brother I said hello." She said, sounding very depressed.

Cam'ren picked right up on her tone and thought it was because he hadn't invited her.

"You can come too. I'd love for you to meet my brother. I haven't seen him in years and we're kinda having a family reunion."

Sunshine wished she could be with Cam'ren at that moment. He was the nicest man that she'd ever been with. It was just that she had other things that she had to deal with.

"I don't think I'll be able to make it. I have some things I need to take care of anyway. You have fun though!"

With that said, Sunshine hung up the phone.

Cam'ren got back to his dorm room and noticed that there were a lot of people whispering in the halls and watching him. He didn't know what all of the gossiping was about, and hoped his brother hadn't gotten into anything.

When he stepped in, Smash and Cam'ron

were waiting for him. They appeared to be having a heated discussion about something that they didn't want him to hear.

"What's up fellas?" Cam'ren asked as he locked his room door.

"Aw, ain't nothing bro. You had some guy come past here looking for yo' chick."

Cam'ren didn't seem to think too much of it.

"Oh! That was probably her brother. I've met him once before."

Cam'ron and Smash looked at each other. It was obvious that Cam'ren didn't understand who or what Ross was. He wasn't in the game so he didn't understand how dangerous a dude like Ross could be.

In Cam'ron's mind, Ross was a serious threat to his little brother and so was Sunshine. He could see that Cam'ren really liked the chick, and so did he, but something had to be done about dude before Cam'ren got caught up in some nut shit.

They were together again after so many years of being apart. Cam'ron didn't want to lose the only person in his life that he could finally call family.

He respected his twin brother for making it. He had dreams. Dreams that Cam'ron might never be able to have because of the hand he was dealt. That didn't mean he didn't want his brother to have a chance at a better life.

The problem with Cam'ren in Cam'ron's

eyes was that he was too naive. He had people all around him that were unscrupulous and who could ruin all the shit that he was working towards.

Cam'ron couldn't let that happen.

"Ay yo', I need to go out for a while. Why don't you get some rest bro. Plus, I gotta make a few calls. You mind if I use yo phone?"

Cam'ren dug in his pocket and gave him the phone as he stepped into the bathroom for a minute while Cam'ren used the bathroom, Cam'ron got Sunshine's number out of his phone then sat the phone back on the night stand by the bed.

He put on his coat and told Smash to get ready to roll out as he waited on his brother.

When Cam'ren came out, he could see that Cam'ron and Smash were ready to leave and wanted to make sure they knew that he planned on taking them to the concert that night, and to the game in the morning.

With that said, they agreed to meet back at his dorm around 6:30 that night to go over to the concert.

Cam'ron and Smash got into Cam'ron's truck. Smash could see that Cam'ron had something on his mind.

"What up my dude? We goin back to the hotel, or what?"

Cam'ron shook his head, "Naw, we gon handle that fat motherfucker before he tries some shit wit my brother about his chick."

"I told you that befo' yo' brother came in! He ain't even dig big dude was his woman's pimp. Yo' brother is slow dude!"

"Naw, it ain't that. He just on some other shit. He ain't never been in the streets like we was. That's why he got all dem dreams and shit. The thing is, if he successful, he might be able to help "us" one day."

"What you mean by dat?" Smash asked not knowing that his brother wanted to be either a prosecutor or a District Attorney.

"He wanna work for the feds or be a Prosecutor. If he stays clean, he can make dat shit happen. That could work out real good as a connect for us Ya' heard?"

Smash started smilin. He understood where Cam'ron's thinking was going. As an organization, they'd have somebody on the inside that could keep them from gettin knocked. He liked it and looked at Cam'ron admiringly.

"Yo', you sharp wit it my dude! So what we gotta do?"

First we gotta find out where this fat pimp lay his head, and I know just who knows where he be."

They drove straight to Amber's house. When they pulled up a block away, Cam'ron used a pay phone on the corner to call the number that Amber had given him the night before.

After a few rings, she picked up and yawned into the phone.

"Hello?"

"Ay yo' Amber! Dis Cam'ron. I need ta holler at you for a minute."

"I was sleepin. Is everything alright?" "Yeah!

Listen, I need some information. You know where dude Ross stay at?"

"Naw! I just started workin at the club. I only seen him with Sunshine. Maybe I can find out from her."

Well I need that information quick. Meet me on the corner of you block in an hour. I'll be in a truck. Ya heard?"

"I'll see what I can do."

"And by the way, remember what I said earlier. Keep dat to yo' for right now. I'll take care of you for the info when you bring it to me."

Smash and Cam'ron got something to eat and then drove around for a while till it was time to meet Amber. They looked for a nice spot to dump her ass off once they got the information.

Leave no witnesses were the rules of the game, and although they both liked her, they ain't wanna leave no loose ends behind.

When it was time to meet Amber, she came out in a pair of high heeled stripper boots, and a lime green mini skirt. Her blond hair was braided back like she was a poor imitation of Bo Derrick. Smash had hit it the night before and Cam'ron wished he had a chance to get a taste himself, but family came first.

Smash got out of the passenger side so that she could scoot in between the two of them and they drove off.

"So what's up my dudes?" She asked as they pulled off down the street.

"You take care a dat for me?"

"Oh yeah! I got it right here! I didn't even have to ask Sunshine. One of my friends knows both of them from the club. She gave me the address."

"Good lookin shawty. You got time for some work? I need to relieve some stress." Cam'ron asked giving her a lustful look.

Smash pulled out a few hundred just to keep her attention as they pulled up behind the abandoned building they'd found.

"Sure! I'da done you for free Daddy!" She said as they came to a stop.

Aiight, we can go right back here, and when I'm done, you can take care of my man."

Amber stepped out of the truck on the passenger side and followed Cam'ren off by the back of the abandoned house. As Cam'ron turned facing her like he was about to unzip his pants, Smash drew his gun and let off three quick shots to the side of Amber's head.

BOP! BOP! BOP!

He followed her body with each shot as she collapsed into a heep. Brain matter stained the old faded cinder block wall taking Amber's thought processes with her life.

Both Cam'ron and Smash got back into their car, then headed away from Amber's neighborhood towards the house that Ross and Sunshine had once shared. When they got there they scoped the place out. It was still pretty early for people who lived their lives making a living in the streets. Cam'ron and Smash checked the back of the house trying to find a way in.

They found an alleyway littered with broken bottles, alley apples, crack vials, and dirty needles.

They worked their way through the overgrown weeds startling rats out of their hiding as they counted the houses until they reached the one that Ross and Sunshine had shared.

Climbing the back fence was a pain in the ass since the gate wasn't completely stable. Once they were over, they peeped into windows to make sure that no one was up.

Seeing that no one was in the back kitchen area, they cracked the back door as quietly as they could with a crow bar they'd brought from the truck. The door popped open with little resistance, and they slid quietly onto the cracked linoleum floor while listening to see if anyone had heard them.

They moved through room after room with guns drawn, and when they were certain that Ross wasn't home, they sat down and waited.

After twenty minutes, they could hear heavy footsteps coming up the old wooden steps of the front porch. Cam'ron and Smash hid on the side of the front hall, just back out of sight in the living room.

That way, as Ross entered the door, he would walk right past them, even if he went up the steps directly across from where they stood.

A key turned in the lock of the front door, then Ross stepped into the front hall. He locked the door, turned, and started coming toward where Smash and Cam'ron waited.

As the massive shadow of Ross grew larger and larger, Smash raised his gun and waited on him, aiming at about Ross' head level.

Ross turned the corner counting the small packets of dope he'd just purchased, and when he looked up to meet Smash's eyes before running into the barrel of the gun, Smash unloaded on him.

BOP! BOP! BOP! BOP! BOP!

In rapid succession shots rang out until you could literally see to the back wall just by staring at where Ross's face used to be.

It took a minute for him to drop, but by then, Smash and Cam'ron were moving out the back alley.

Within minutes they were back in their car and heading in another direction as Smash drove and Cam'ron thumbed through a phone book looking for real estate agents.

****

Troy sat in the upper bleachers of a Scott Branch Home Game. He had a few of his young killers with him as he sat like a don, all icy, to impress the young girls that sat admiring him.

Tamara; his number one, sat watching

"him" and daring any of the young girls "he" watched to get stupid. Tamara was only about 5'6" and weighed no more than 137 pounds. What she lacked in size she made up for in heart. That's why Troy loved her so much. She was a rider and he got off on seeing her punish the other girls who dared to chase after him. It was a game for him, pure and simple, and he loved to push the limits.

He looked back over his shoulder at Tamara sitting with her sister Rita, and her daughter Smallworld.

Rita was just the opposite of her feisty sister. Rita was quiet, but big. She weighed nearly 260 pounds and stood 5'10". She didn't say much, but anything Tamara got into, Rita had her back.

Smallworld had just turned 14 and was starting to blossom into her womanhood. Troy had started messing with her mother Tamara at that same age, and often looked at Smallworld with lust in his heart.

As he turned back around to finish watching the game, a dude from his team slammed on Sumter.

Troy yelled with the onlookers, "Oh Shit! What? What? Das how you do it baby!"

As he sat back down his phone rang. "Yo' who dis?"

"It's yo' father fool! Where you at?"

"I'm at the game Pops. I got money on my team!" He yelled to be heard over the cheers of the crowd.

"You got that message I left for you. So why you ain't out taken care a dat!

His father was on some other shit. He wanted Troy to take Cam'ron out and take over his connect so that they could run all the drugs. What his father didn't know was that Cam'ron wasn't in town and that Troy was waiting for him to come back. Plus, he couldn't very well kill Cam'ron himself. He had to get somebody to do it for him so that it wouldn't lead back to him.

It was a tricky situation. If Cam'ron knew he was trying to hire someone to kill him, then he'd be dead and stinkin himself. He just had to bide his time and set everything up right.

"I'm on it Pop. I can't just do this shit at the drop of a dime. Plus, he ain't even in town right now!"

He could tell that his father was losing his patience by the quiet on the other end of the line.

"Just make sure you handle yo' business. I'll see you at the house later."

With the conversation ended, Troy hung up the phone. He had money on the game and was hoping the Sumter cats got out of line so he could take his frustration out on them. They'd stomped out one of his young bucks at their last game, so that gave him even more reason to vent on them if they gave him a reason.

As the game ended, Troy spotted one of his young freaks heading out to the parking lot. He got up and tried to lose Tamara in the crowd as he ducked out to holler at her.

Tamara was distracted after the game trying to clean up the Slurpy juice Smallworld had spilled all over her clothes. When she looked up, Troy was nowhere to be found.

She tried to scan the crowd of people as they moved to leave the game and didn't see him, so she decided to try and head him off at his truck.

She knew he had money on the game and intended to get a piece of the money so she could go shopping, and then clubbing later on afterwards.

She moved as fast as she could through the throng of people trying to make her way to the parking lot with Smallworld and Rita in tow.

She looked for Troy's truck and couldn't see it at first, so she picked up the pace and moved further into the lot behind the courts. As she turned the corner, she spotted Troy leaning on his truck with the door open, talking to some young chicken head. Tamara was flaming and had come prepared for just such an occasion.

Tamara kept a pair of sneakers and petroleum jelly in her bag in case she had to beat a bitch down. Most of the young girls had learned a long time ago to stay out of Troy's face after the woman had beat them down.

Tamara pulled off her shoes and dug out her sneakers, smeared Vaseline on her face, and made her way towards where Troy stood talking to the high school hoochie that was talking to her man. As she came around the truck, she could see that there were a few other females standing there waiting on the girl as she wrote down her number for Troy.

As Troy looked up and saw Tamara coming, he smiled like he was innocently having a conversation with the young lady.

Tamara didn't say a word. She dropped her purse 2 steps before she got to the girl and started raining blows like a mad woman.

Troy slid out of the truck and out of the way as he smiled and watched Tamara hit the young girl with three upper cuts while she pulled her head down to meet her fist.

Out of the corner of his eye he saw another girl step in and start whaling on Tamara from the side. Tamara was caught off guard and took the full brunt of the girl's blows to her face.

As she went down, the other girl continued to beat and stomp Tamara, knocking the wind out of her.

Rita pushed past Troy like a linebacker and was on the other girl in seconds. She punched the girl in mid swing of hitting her sister with a hay maker that knocked the girl out!

Everybody in the crowd OOOOHED as the girl went down. Rita continued to punch the girl with her back to the rest of her friends. This continued for a few seconds before another girl stepped up behind Rita and hit her in the head with something. Blood splashed on the concrete as a loud thunk! Could be heard when the girl hit her.

She drew back again and Troy could see that the girl had a pad lock hooked to her belt as an improvised club. She beat down on Rita and Tamara like a wild woman as blood sprayed everywhere.

Troy sat back enjoying the show. He enjoyed seeing people hurt, it allowed him to let off steam when he was mad, and he was mad at all the shit that was happening in his life at that time.

He was so distracted by what he was watching that he didn't notice Smallworld reach under the seat of his truck, or when she turned and aimed at the woman reigning down blows on her aunt and mother. The explosion of the bullet out of the barrel startled him as he felt the wind of the bullet brush against his jacket.

Boom! The gun went off and everybody scattered. The big chick that was beating her aunt and mother with the lock hit the sand and gravel parking lot like a sack of potatoes with half of her head missing.

The crowd scattered and Troy looked back expecting death to come to him as well. When he turned, Smallworld was standing there holding his 40 caliber, with tears running down her face.

Troy grabbed the gun from the little girl and pulled her up into the back cab of his Cadillac truck. He started the engine and pulled off leaving Tamara and Rita to get home the best way that they could.

He pulled out of the school with the other cars and stopped by one of his young bucks who was walking to his car. He wiped the gun down on his shirt, then threw the gun in a paper bag. He hollered for the young buck to come over and instructed him to ditch the gun as he handed it to him.

The youngster knew the drill and grabbed the gun while he kept walking like nothing ever happened.

Troy pulled off and started driving casually like he didn't just see someone get murdered. He looked over at Smallworld who'd stopped crying. She looked like she was lost and Troy didn't know if she'd lost her mind after what she'd just done.

"You okay girl?" He asked her after she didn't say anything.

She looked at him like she was some place far away at first. Then, slowly she nodded her head.

"You did what you had to do! Don't go feelin sorry fo' dat ho'! She coulda kilt yo' Mamma. Ya heard me?"

"Yeah!" Smallworld answered in her little girl's voice.

"My Momma gonna be okay?" She asked after a while.

"Hell Yeah!" Troy answered. He knew Tamara. They'd grown up together. She wasn't gonna rat on her own daughter and neither was anybody else. People knew Troy and the people he messed with.

It was gonna be another unsolved murder of a young black girl in the South. Plain and simple.

Troy tried to make the little girl feel better about what she'd done.

"You know, you a killer now! Ain't nobody gonna mess wit you no more. Shit, you could get money for doin that kinda shit!"

"How?" Smallworld asked.

Troy looked at her with a sideways grin as a plan started forming in his mind.

"Shit! you could do a few hits for me!"

Smallworld didn't even seem phased by what Troy said. She was a child and didn't grasp what he was talking about completely.

All she thought about was the money and how she could buy new stuff with the money like her Mom did.

"How much you gon give me if I do?"

Troy could tell she was really interested, so he shot some numbers at her.

"You could make $500.00 a head doin that. That's good money!" Troy lied, knowing it was more like $5,000.00 and up to do a hit, but Smallworld was too young to know that.

Smallworld got excited at the possibility of making that kind of money. Thinking about the money took away her worries about her mother and her aunt. It made her forget how she felt after pulling the trigger. It wasn't quite like the video games she'd played, but she liked the fact that everybody was scared of her.

"When you want me to do it again?" She asked Troy.

Troy smiled like a mad man.

"Don't worry, I'll call you when I need you. Matter fact, here's a down payment! He dug into his pocket and handed her all the money he had. It was chump change to him. He was a millionaire.

He pulled up in front of Tamara's house to drop Smallworld off. Just as she went to get out, he stopped her.

"Look here Baby girl. This between me and you. Don't tell nobody what just happened back there or what we talked about. This is our little secret! You don't wanna go to jail and you don't want yo' Momma to go to jail either. So keep yo mouth shut and er' thang 'll be alright. Tell yo' momma I'ma call her. And don't say nothin about what we just talked about. Ya heard?"

Smallworld looked scared. Troy had a nasty look in his eyes when he warned her to quiet. She nodded her head, stuffed the money in her pocket, and went in the house.

CHAPTER 12

Cam'ron and Smash exited the realtor's office at about 11:30 a.m. Smash jumped into the driver's seat again as Cam'ron started thumbing through the yellow pages for car dealerships. Once he found what he was looking for, he gave Smash the directions and they pulled up to the dealership minutes later.

Trucks and cars of every color and size littered the lot. Smash put out his Dutch and exited the vehicle with Cam'ron. They walked down the rows of cars and trucks until Cam'ron stopped in front of a Black Yukon Denali that stood completely kitted up. Smash started noddin his head unconsciously as Cam'ron took a lap around the huge truck, examining the interior, and checking to see if the door was unlocked.

A dealer walked over, "Can I help you gentlemen?"

Cam'ron looked him up and down, then asked, "How much?"

The dealer started ringing his hands uncertain about how much he could get on commission and still cut a deal.

"A completely kitted truck like this costs a pretty penny. You sure you gentlemen can handle the payments on something like this?"

Smash bust out laughing. "Payments? We pay cash my Dude!"

The man saw dollar signs immediately and invited them into the dealership where they could negotiate. Within minutes the truck had dealer's tags and was rolling behind Cam'ron's truck down the highway en route back to the new condo Cam'ron had just bought for his brother off of Georgetown Avenue.

As he drove he clicked open the cell phone and dialed Sunshine's number he'd gotten out of his brother's phone. Sunshine was still asleep and hiding out in Amber's room when she picked up.

"Hello?" She asked not recognizing the number.

"Ay Sunshine, this Cam'ren's brother. I know he told you we just hooked up and I know we ain't never meant before (he lied) but we havin a surprise party for Cam'ren and I'd like for you to come."

"How'd you get my number?" Sunshine asked suspiciously.

"I got it off my brother's phone. Now listen, catch a cab to this address. The people at the front desk will have a set of keys for you. Make yo self comfortable and we'll be there around 5:30 tonight. Oh! And wear somethin nice!"

With that, Cam'ron turned onto the campus and parked in front of his brother's dorm.

Smash pulled up and parked right beside

him as all the students who were milling about checked out the new ride that Smash had just parked.

They both gave dap to each other as they headed inside and up to Cam'ren's room.

When they knocked, a still half sleep Cam'ren answered the door in his boxers and a tee shirt.

Cam'ron smiled. His brother liked to sleep the same way he did. They'd been sleeping in boxers and a tee shirt since they were kids.

"What up my dude?" Smash greeted as they both stepped into Cam'ren's room.

Cam'ren yawned as he stretched, "What time is it?"

Cam'ron checked his watch. "It's 4:30 Dawg. Time to get up! I got a surprise fo you!"

Cam'ren looked at his brother and how excited he was as Smash puffed on his Dutch and started smiling behind the smoke.

"What da hell are you two up to?"

"Come on man! We need to do some quick shoppin. We got a date! Plus, I got a few surprises for ya, ya heard?"

Cam'ren didn't argue with his brother. He seemed in a really good mood. He went in and got dressed. While he was doing that, Cam'ron got on the phone to let the realtor know they could give the keys to Sunshine and let her know to wait at the new Condo he'd bought for his brother to stay in.

After a few minute's, Cam'ren came out in another preppy Polo outfit like the one he'd worn the night before, only in a different color.

Smash immediately bust out laughin. "Yo my dude! Why you keep wearin that garbage?"

Cam'ren started to justify what he was wearing and thought better of it. When Cam'ron saw his brother's feelings was kinda hurt, he stepped in.

"Don't even worry bout it bro! I'm about to hook you up! Let's hit the strip, we ain't got that much time!"

With that said, Cam'ron stepped to his brother and handed him a set of keys.

Cam'ron looked at him kinda puzzled. "We takin your truck or do you want me to drive the car?"

Cam'ron smiled, "Naw dawg, we taken your truck! Follow me!"

Cam'ron led his brother out the dorm room door and out into the parking lot. He'd seen his brother's truck and Cam'ron noticed how much he liked it. What he saw sittin next to it was just as nice!

Cam'ron led him over to the Yukon and Cam'ren just stood there speechless. "Dis fo' you bro! Congratulations man!"

Cam'ren turned around and hugged his brother with tears in his eyes. Everybody in front of the dorm looked on with envy.

Smash gave Cam'ren some dap and a hug too, then Cam'ron rushed them both into the truck so they could go shopping before his next surprise.

They shopped for like 30 minutes straight. Once Cam'ron knew his brother's sizes, him and Smash went on a speed shopping spree for themselves and Cam'ren. The sky was the limit. Anything Cam'ron saw that he wanted he bought it with his Platinum Card he'd acquired through his legitimate business fronts.

They left the store in all new gear and shot straight to a high rise off of Georgetown Avenue.

Cam'ren had only been in this part of D.C. when he was visiting Nancy at the condo that her parent's had given her off campus. He didn't like staying over at her place since it made him feel guilty about the things he couldn't provide for her. She was a rich spoiled whore who got everything from her mother and father, while Cam'ren was an adopted child.

He knew his parents loved him and gave him the best that they could, but they weren't rich.

As Cam'ron instructed Cam'ren on where to park, he wondered who they had come to see.

They got into the chrome and glass elevators and rode all the way to the top floor. When they stepped off the elevator, they found the front door of the Penthouse ajar with music blasting out of the stereo.

Cam'ren looked over at Cam'ren with the, "What the hell is going on face," as they stepped to the half open door. Cam'ren pushed the door all the way open and Cam'ren almost lost his mind when he saw Sunshine dancing on the couches like a kid at a sleep over party.

"What the hell?" Were the only words Cam'ren could get out of his mouth before Sunshine jumped down off the couch and ran straight into Cam'ren's arms. She kissed him deeply and was so excited she didn't even notice Cam'ron and Smash standing right behind Cam'ren in the hall.

"I love you baby! Thank you! Thank you!"

She said as tears of joy crawled out of her eyes.

Cam'ren just stood there stunned and taking it all in. When she was calm, he pushed Sunshine back and said, "Baby, I'd like for you to meet my brother. He did all of this."

As he said it, he stepped to the side so that Sunshine could see Cam'ron and Smash standing in the hall. She vaguely remembered seeing Smash at Amber's house, but wasn't sure. What distracted her most was the uncanny resemblance that Cam'ren shared with his brother. For a moment she had to do a double take because she thought her mind was playing tricks on her.

Cam'ron stepped up and gave Sunshine a hug, then said, "Sorry I had to be so secretive Shawty, but I'm glad to see y'all found your place."

Sunshine looked at him real suspicious, like the way he talked seemed familiar to her. She didn't want to say anything in front of Cam'ren, and Cam'ron gave her a look that let her know something was up.

She shook his hand and was introduced to Smash. After the greetings, they all walked into the Condo and Cam'ron gave them the tour before handing over two sets of keys to them. One set to Sunshine, and one set to Cam'ren.

Cam'ren was in heaven and Sunshine seemed to be just as happy for him. Cam'ron asked if he could talk to Sunshine for a minute out on the terrace, and they both excused themselves.

When they were alone, Cam'ron ran things down to her. "Listen Sunshine, I know all about your situation and your secret is safe wit me. You won't have no more problems outta Ross neither. So what bro don't know won't hurt em'. Ya Heard?"

Sunshine let out a breath of fresh air. She didn't know what to expect. She didn't know if this was some type of sick joke or not. She was just glad to have a chance at a better life.

"I hope you know I really meant what I just told your brother, and I'ma try to make him happy. I don't know how or why you did all this for me, but thank you!"

She started crying and hugged Cam'ron as he smiled proudly looking out over the skyline of D.C.

He'd made himself a family and he intended to keep it. To see his brother happy meant everything to him, and knowing that he'd also helped somebody as sweet as Sunshine made him feel even better when he compared some of the evil he'd had to do to get to where he was.

As he hugged Sunshine, Cam'ren and Smash came onto the balcony with drinks and they all toasted to Cam'ron and Cam'ren.

After that, it was on and popping. They pulled up to the Jay-Z Concert. The place was jumpin like crazy. You could hear the bass kick of the Concert speakers from 10 blocks away as all of Howard University converged on the concert. Fly girls wore booty shorts, and ballers cruised in freshly detailed cars looking for a young hotty to take home.

Sunshine and Cam'ren followed Smash and Cam'ron in their new truck and fresh gear. They were living the life as it was meant to be. They pulled up and parked as the young girls gave Smash and Cam'ron the hot in the ass eyes.

Smash made his way over to a crowd of girls and started playing for a cutey's number as Cam'ron waited. He looked back and watched as Sunshine and Cam'ren made their way into the concert. While he watched, sneaky assed Nancy came up behind him and grabbed him from behind.

"Hey Cam'ron! Fancy meeting you here!"

Cam'ron turned around to see Nancy leathered down in all Gucci with a pair of matching frames and purse. She even had a matching bandana with Gucci symbols on it pulling her hair back into curls.

Nancy looked hot as hell in the outfit, and the camel toe was making it's presence known, the leather suit was so tight.

She tried to kiss Cam'ron and he turned his head away. He wasn't that caught up, and Nancy stepped back, obviously hurt.

"So now you don't wanna kiss me Cam'ron! That's right! I said Cam'ron! I know the difference between you two now."

Smash stayed over by the group of chicks he was talking to, watching the whole scene go down and laughing.

"Yo' Shawty! Why you makin a scene? I came out to have fun tonight. I ain't come up here to fight. Why don't you give me yo' number and I'll call you later before I leave."

Nancy calmed down and took his phone to put her number in. She smiled over at Smash, then back at Cam'ron, "You better call me!" Then left.

The rest of the night was enjoyable. The brothers enjoyed themselves throughout the entire evening. In the morning they went to the Home Coming game. Cam'ron stepped off to have another freak session one on one with Nancy before he left.

He had one more surprise for his brother and Sunshine that he dropped before returning home. They were all at the condo and hugging each other while saying their good byes. Cam'ron pulled his brother to the side and gave him a title and another set of keys.

Cam'ren looked at his brother puzzled.

"What's this for bro?"

Cam'ren smiled, "Well you ain't gon be in college forever. So when you decide you ready to settle down and come home. You'll have a place to stay. I had my girl Pam secure something special for you. She's dying to meet you both by the way. Whenever you get done here, come on home."

With final hugs exchanged all around, Smash and Camron hit the road. The family reunion was over and it was time to get back to business!

CHAPTER 13

Cam'ron jumped on the E-Way with Smash driving. It was a 10½ hour drive to get back to Sumter, South Carolina. On the ride back, they had a lot to talk about.

"First things first, my dude. We gotta check in wit da Ole Heads. I know they ready to re-up." Smash said after a puff of his signature Dutch.

"I'ma call Drag and June. We can make that drop befo' we get settled," Cam'ron said as he flipped open his cellular."

After three rings, Drag picked up. "Whas happenin Baby! Who dis?" Drag answered on some smooth, fly, old school lingo.
Everything about Drag was fly. That's why Cam'ron liked him so much. Drag knew how to run them streets. He'd been doin it for years with his partner June.

They had every project and housing complex moving product. If it was in The South, Drag could move it through his connections in the streets.

That made June and Drag King Pins. They bought 20 Kilos a week at $25,000 a brick. When they stepped on the weight they got, they doubled the money they made selling it on the streets.

That they were getting all of their product

from Cam'ron, meant that they had exclusive control of the entire South's drug trade while Cam'ron made 2 million a month in steady money. This had gone on since Cam'ron was a young buck. Now him and his squad were filthy rich.

"Was up Drag? It's Cam'ron. I'm on my way in. What y'all need?"

"We only got a quarter tank on gas baby! We gonna have to fill it up!" That let Cam'ron know they were down to their last 5 bricks of product and would be out soon. They needed more weight.

"I'm on my way. Meet me at the spot!"

"Okay, be safe Baby! I'll see you when you get in!" Drag said in his wheezing voice. Drag always talked like he was on syrup or drunk. Cam'ron clicked shut the phone, turned to Smash and said, "We gotta go to the stash house first. They almost sold out of da product baby."

Smash looked over at Cam'ron with a smile on his face. "Dat also mean we get ta count more money!" Then put his foot to the floor so they could get there sooner.

When they pulled up to the stash spot, Shamroc answered the door with a stick of Ghanga hangin out his mouth on some true Rastafarian shit.

They loaded up twenty kilos of cocaine in Saran wrapped bricks, then headed over to the drop spot in the woods.

The two old men sat in front of an old trailer

back in the woods with a barbecue grill on the lawn, reclining in folding lawn chairs.

They both leaned forward with their stubby and aged legs kicked out, heels up, their hands resting on wooden canes. They each had a toothpick hanging out of their mouth like most black Southern gentlemen.

Cam'ron and Smash walked up on the old heads and hugged them. It was 1:30 a.m. in the morning and they were sittin up waiting on them for the drop.

They'd been moving 20 bricks a week for Cam'ron since he first made his connection to them through Smash.

In exchange, Cam'ron picked up two body sized bags of money and loaded them into the back of his truck.

They didn't do much talking. There wasn't much to be said except that he'd check back in soon.

There was never any problem with the product, and Drag, and June were always like clockwork with the money. That's what made everything run smooth.

Before Cam'ron left, Drag and June called him back for a minute as Smash climbed into the passenger seat.

"Before you leave man, I gotta have a talk wit you Caam," Drag said as Cam'ron stepped to get in his truck."

Drag walked up to meet Cam'ron as he came back across the lawn. "I don't like to get in people's business man, but you need ta watch ya man Troy," Drag said as he took the tooth out of his mouth. June nodded in agreement as he leaned over his cane.

"He let that little girl get shot over his dumb shit!"

"What you talkin bout Drag?"

Cam'ron didn't know anything about the situation with Troy's girl since he'd been out of town.

Drag explained everything that happened to Cam'ron, and when he was done, he let it be known that the streets wasn't feeling what happened.

The young girl Ruby gettin killed by Smallworld because of some dumb shit that Troy did was foul.

It was on the news and could draw serious heat to the streets. Especially since useless killings were never good business.

Cam'ron thanked Drag for the info and rolled out. He would have to get with Troy about what took place.

But first, he had to go home....

****

The relationship with Pam and Cam'ron was difficult for the next few days. Cam'ron had a lot of catching up to do in his business affairs, and that distracted him from his relationship with Pam.

The night he got home, Pam played too tired to give him any pussy, so he left her alone.

When Cam'ron was up and in the house, she was doing paperwork trying to keep up with running the Realty Office they owned.

They'd hardly even talked about what Cam'ron did with his brother. It was like she was distant from him and trying to avoid him.

He called Troy so they could do a tally on the money they'd collected at the stash house.

When Troy came to pick him up, he didn't even wanna come into the house. He just waited for Cam'ron outside in the driveway.

The vibe seemed funny with Troy. Troy didn't seem like himself. As they rode, they hardly talked. It was all business, and not the family vibe they used to share.

It pissed Cam'ron off, and as he took a break from counting the money, he asked Troy what was up. "Ay yo my dude! You been real quiet. You aiight man?"

Troy looked over at Cam'ron with a suspicious look on his face.

"What you mean by that?" Troy asked as he looked back at Cam'ron.

"I'm sayin, what's been goin on while I was outta town?"

"Ain't nothin goin on. What are you talkin bout Cam'ron?"

Cam'ron leaned back in the kitchen chair with all the money in front of him in stacks.

"Damn my dude, I heard about the shootin

after da game."

Cam'ron said with a smirk on his face while he rubbed his chin hairs.

"Oh, that wasn't bout nothing." Troy answered on the defensive. Cam'ron didn't think so.

"That ain't what I heard!"

Troy got up like he had an attitude, "So what the fuck did yo' ass hear then?" He said with his face all broken up.

Cam'ron looked at him with serious suspicion by the way Troy had changed in just a few days. Somethin was up!

"Why you gettin mad my dude? I'm jus tryna let you know what I heard. Word is, Tamara finally got what her hand called for. But the fucked up part about it is, the girl Ruby got killed by her daughter wit yo' gun! How you let a little girl get yo gun?"

Troy couldn't deny that. "Yeah, she did, but dat little bitch Ruby deserved it! That's why she ain't breathin!"

Ruby was a 16 year old girl who had just gotten out of juvenile hall. She'd learned the belt and pad lock trick there. The other girl that Tamara had beat up for talking to Troy was her cousin and she was only sixteen. He was a grown man messing with kids. The shit just ain't look good. Then, to have had somebody killed over it made the community upset since everybody liked Ruby. She was born and raised in Sumter and Troy wasn't!

What Cam'ron didn't know about Troy and was just starting to suspect was that he might be a child molester too. He didn't need that kind of person in his organization.

As he thought about this, Smash came at him.

"I bet yo' chick will think twice before beaten up on a little kid over you!" Stated Smash as he sat counting the money with them. He was laughing when he said it! He was also mad because he knew little Ruby since she was a baby.

Troy looked over at Smash with hate and envy in his eyes. "So now you niggahs wanna judge me?"

Smash just kept laughin at him as he puffed on his Dutch and gave him the hard grit. He wanted to fuck Troy up on G.P. He just never liked him. Smash was geographical just like Troy. He just tried not to bring it around Cam'ron. They were taking care of other business.

When Troy saw Smash wouldn't feed because of Cam'ron, he tried to push the issue about Smash laughin at him.

"Dawg, errthing funny to yo' ass my Dude?" Cam'ron could see that Troy was getting heated. He was going into a real heavy southern accent as he talked. Smash was gettin under his skin. He was ready to jump on Smash's ass.

"Get Money" by Biggie Smalls came through Cam'ron's phone as his ringtone just when the two of them were about to go at it.

It was Nancy!

Cam'ron got up as Smash and Troy kept the grits hot with each other, then answered the phone.

"Hey handsome!" Nancy yelled from way down in D.C.

Cam'ron didn't wanna talk to her. He tried to brush her off.

He'd only been gone a few days and she was starting to get clingy.

"I'm kinda busy right now. Can I call you back?" He said impatiently.

Nancy started pouting on the phone like a spoiled kid. She was a nympho who always wanted attention and Cam'ron didn't have time for her games. He hung up on her and looked back at his squad.

"Yo, y'all need to chill wit that shit! Let's finish countin this money. We can sit down over dinner tomorrow night and talk about it! My place tomorrow at 5:30."

Cam'ron wanted to keep things cool in the squad. Too many things were happening on a personal level for him to have to worry about in-fighting. He didn't know if Troy had really been messing with any of the young girls. So he gave him the benefit of the doubt.

The ill will he was having for Smash was probably because they'd been spending so much time together.

They'd known each other for too long on the business side, and growing up, for things to get too heated.

They agreed and finished counting the money.

****

Cam'ren took his final exam the Tuesday after Cam'ron left. He'd done his best and probably better than most. Cam'ren always stayed on his studying habits. His adopted parents had instilled discipline in him when it came to studying.

He'd be taking the bar within the coming weeks to finally secure a law degree. Then there'd be nothing left but the graduation ceremony. He still hadn't heard anything back on his F.B.I. application.

Since he had a few weeks off, he decided to surprise his brother and come to see him at "his" home.

Sunshine had settled into living with him and playing wifey. She was like a kid who was living a dream. Just to be able to wake up next to her made Cam'ren happy.

That she wanted to join him and pick out furniture for the other home in Sumter made Cam'ren even happier. They left at 10:00 a.m. so that they could get there kind of early that night.

As Cam'ren drove, Sunshine went through her magazines and catalogs, asking Cam'ren what he liked as she got ready to do the interior of their second home.

What she didn't know was that Cam'ren was considering marrying her and wanted to do it in front of his family.

That Thursday evening, Cam'ron, Cam'ren, and Smash sat at Cam'ron's house eating dinner. Pam cooked, and the tension between her and Troy was almost palpable.

Pam pretty much stayed in the kitchen as they talked at the table. She served them each a plate covered with home cooked food, then stayed back in the kitchen.

While Cam'ron, Smash, and Troy started discussing the problem from the day before, the phone rang again. When Cam'ron excused himself for some privacy, he saw that it was another call from Nancy. It was the tenth time she'd called that day!

"Yo', why you keep callin me? You blowin up my phone! I got a wifey!" Cam'ron answered as he took the call.

Nancy went ballistic. "I'm your wifey niggah. That's why you was fuckin me. I thought we had a relationship?"

Cam'ron let air out of his mouth like he was impersonating a flat tire. "Yo', I'm in da middle of some business. Lose my number!"

Just when he was about to hang up on her she yelled into the phone, "Cam'ron wait! I'm pregnant!"

Cam'ron thought maybe he'd heard wrong since he didn't have his ear all the way to the phone, he was about to hang up. He opened the phone back up and put it back to his ear.

"What the fuck did you just say?"

"I said I'm pregnant Cam'ron, and your the father!"

Cam'ron nearly lost it!

"Bitch is you crazy? What the hell you talkin about I'm the Daddy! You lost your mind?"

Nancy started giggling like a goofy school girl. She was on some other shit.

"You're the only person that I was with. At least that's what I'm gonna tell my father. You know he's a District Court judge right?"

Nancy was threatening him. Her father could use his pull with the feds to start asking a lot of questions he didn't want answered. Cam'ron was always on point about the feds and snitches. He didn't need that.

"Nancy, I'ma have to think about this. I need some time to figure out what we gonna do. Just be cool baby and I'll be riiight der!" Cam'ron told her as he started puttin a plan together to get rid of the little bitch.

When he hung up and walked back into the living room, he tried to hide the worried look on his face as Pam cleared the table, but Smash caught it. When Pam walked out, Smash leaned into him at the table, "Why da long face my dude?"

"We gotta take a trip back down D.C."

Pam heard him as she walked back in to get the rest of the plates.

"Damn, you leavin me again baby?"

Troy looked at her with hate and a, "I told you so," look on his face.

Cam'ron turned and tried to explain, "Yeah! I have some business that I need to take care of."

"How long this time?" Pam asked with an attitude.

Pam heard him on the phone, and by the sound of his voice, she knew it was another female.

"A few days this time." Cam'ron said while looking over at her.

He knew that his trips were getting on her nerves. What he didn't know was that his trips had caused her to stray with Troy.

Troy got up to give them some privacy. He stepped out of the dining room heading toward the front veranda. When he was outside he dialed Smallworld's number and waited for an answer.

"Hello," Smallworld answered.

"Baby Girl, it's me! I need you to handle what we talked about." He whispered into the phone.

"What you need me to do?"

"Meet me down the street from your house in an hour."

He hung up ending the call, and was tucking his phone into his pocket just as Smash came out to smoke a Dutch.

As he looked over at Smash, neither one of them had any conversation for each other. It was obvious that Troy couldn't stand Smash, and Smash couldn't stand him. In Smash's mind, he was jealous of him and his relationship with Cam'ron.

There were parts of the business that only Smash and Cam'ron shared. Plus, Troy wasn't interested in Real Estate or any of the other businesses Cam'ron and Smash invested their money into.

Troy was a drug dealer, plain and simple. As a youth, when Cam'ron got the connect, it was just Cam'ron and Troy. They were supposed to be partners with Troy using his connections through his father's organization to move his end of the weight.

He had his own distribution, and they split the money fifty/fifty.

As the organization grew, Troy felt like Smash was where "he" was supposed to be. Cam'ron got hooked up with Drag and June to move the weight and pretty much cut off the hook up he had with his father Mickey's people to move the weight.

Cam'ron didn't know that was how he was doing it since Mickey had been in and out of the feds over the last few years for racketeering charges. When he got out, he assumed his son Troy was still holding things down.

When he wasn't getting payments from his distribution of coke through Troy anymore, he decided to take his shit and kill him like he'd done to Cam'ron's father P-Love.

Troy had grown attached to Cam'ron, but that was only until he started fuckin with Pam.

That made his jealousy of Cam'ron grow to the point that he thought Cam'ron only looked at him like a flunky instead of his homie and partner.

If Cam'ron would've put him on the connect, he would've killed him a long time ago. He was tired of hiding who he was and who his father was. He wanted him dead just as much as his father did now. He just couldn't kill him until he was in with the connect. A connect Cam'ron kept to himself.

If he could make Cam'ron's death look like an accident, he was hoping he could step over and take his half of the business with his death having no connection to him.

His father was tired of waiting on him to get it done, and he intended to his way, by killing three birds with one stone.

He was gonna get Pam for disrespecting him and killing his baby, Smash for disrespecting him and taking a position with Cam'ron that should've been his, and Cam'ron for treating him like a flunky all these years.

As he stood in front of Cam'ron's sprawling mansion hating all the success he'd gained, Cam'ron came out onto the veranda with a bag filled with guns and some clothes to cover them up. He tossed Smash the keys to his truck and Smash moved off to pull the truck up out of the garage.

As Smash left, Cam'ron turned to Troy, "Yo' my dude. I'm sorry I gotta leave. We never really got to have our talk like we should have. I'ma get at you when I come back though. You gon be aiight?"

Troy came over and gave Cam'ron some dap like he always did. "It's cool brah! We gon work it out. We always do! Ya heard?"

I'll get at you in a few days so we can re-up on our weight. I just filled the tanks so the streets should be cool til I come back."

Troy looked at Cam'ron with a serious face. "If you gave me the connect, I could handle that business."

Cam'ron just laughed at him. "Naw man! I got it baby. Every thang is cool where it's at. I'll talk to you later!" Then, he climbed into the truck heading back to D.C.

The ride was long, and what Cam'ron didn't know was that his brother had passed him on the other side of the highway, coming to see him with Sunshine....

CHAPTER 14

When Cam'ren and Sunshine pulled into the front entrance of Good Estates, they were flabbergasted. They both looked at the sprawling piece of land that Cam'ren's brother owned.

Houses stood in various stages of development as far as the eyes could see. They both looked at each other with a shocked expression on their faces. They knew that Cam'ron said he was a real estate broker, but they had no idea of the magnitude of what he owned.

Cam'ren reached over to check the navigation system to see if they were at the right place. When it came up correctly, they continued to follow the path set by the truck's G.P.S.

Cam'ron's home sat on a hill overlooking the entire development of property. It was like a castle looking out over the lesser houses. As they drove up, they looked at the various for sale signs reading "Good Real Estate" that stood in front of the twenty development driveways that they passed to get to Cam'ron's Mansion.

They pulled up to a newly completed House that had the same address as the title that Cam'ron gave them. Cam'ren stopped in front of the freshly laid driveway that led up to the new home that sat across from his brother's Mansion.

"Should we check out our new house or see Cam'ron first?"

Cam'ren asked Sunshine as she looked at their second home. "It's too late to really see it, plus it doesn't have furniture. Let's go see your brother first, then we can see the house in the morning."

Cam'ren kept going up to the entrance of Cam'ron's home and pushed the call button at the front of the wrought iron gates that led into Cam'ron's long driveway.

A female voice came over the speaker. "Who is it?"

"Surprise!" Cam'ren and Sunshine yelled from the truck.

"Who is this?" Pam asked obviously irritated.

"It's us! Cam'ren and Sunshine! Is my brother Cam'ron here?"

"Hold on!" The female voice answered. As they waited, a camera turned into their direction. Cam'ren noticed it and stepped out of his truck, so the person looking at him through the camera could get a good look.

Pam came back through the intercom. "Drive up!" She said as the gates opened.

When they pulled up, Pam was there to greet them. She looked at Cam'ren and was caught off guard by how much Cam'ren and Cam'ron looked alike. She walked straight up to him and hugged him.

"I've heard so much about you! What are you doing here?"

"We wanted to surprise y'all." Cam'ren beamed proudly.

"Does Cam'ron know y'all are coming?"

"Nope!" Cam'ren answered with a sly grin on his face.

"Well, he ain't here. He just went out of town!"

Cam'ren and Sunshine looked heart broken. "Well, we'll just have to go and stay at our house then."

Pam wasn't trying to hear any of that. "No you won't! You don't even have any furniture in the place! Y'all will stay here.

"I just finished your paperwork to transfer everything into your names and the place was just finished up yesterday. Besides, we've got plenty of rooms!"

Sunshine had been quiet the whole time as she watched the exchange, and because Cam'ren hadn't introduced her to Pam.

As Pam grabbed Cam'ren by the arm, he realized that Sunshine was standing back away from the two of them since Cam'ren hadn't properly introduced her to Pam.

Cam'ren looked back, "Oh! I'm sorry baby. Pam this is my girl Sunshine. Sunshine, this is Pam."

Sunshine stepped up shyly, "Pleased to meet you!"

Pam stepped to her and hugged her. "Girl

you ain't gotta be all proper wit me! We practically sisters! Now come on and let's get y'all settled!"

They went into the house and looked around at the lush interior of Cam'ron's home. It was like being in a museum. Pam showed them around the place until she noticed that they looked tired after their long drive.

"Listen, I have to make a run to the front office to pick up some paperwork my mother left for me to take care of. We've got one of our first estates in escrow, y'all get comfortable while I take care of that. I should be back in about an hour or so. Will you two be okay?"

It was nearly 9:00 and Cam'ren wanted to still have a talk with his parents about his marrying Sunshine. He decided to get it out of the way now before it got too late.

"Listen Sunshine, I'm gonna run over to my parent's house.

"Will you be okay till I get back?"

Sunshine looked around in the house and said, "I hope I don't get lost in here!"

Pam and Cam'ren laughed before Pam said, "Make yourself at home. I'll be back as soon as I can."

They both walked out as Pam went over to her Bentley GT and climbed in. Cam'ren followed her out to the front of the development, then drove 20 minutes to his adopted parents' home.

He never noticed Troy's car parked two developments over from Cam'ron's house, since it was parked in the back with the lights off.

Smallworld sat inside listening to Troy as he wrote down the security codes and instructions on how to get into Cam'ron's house.

When Troy was certain that she knew how to get in, he let her out of the passenger side, and let her know he'd be waiting for her there when she was done.

Smallworld made her way through the 2 construction sites toward the rear of Cam'ron's house. She came up to the back patio, then slowly made her way up to the massive deck that hung from the entire back of the house.

Off to the side she could see an Olympic sized pool surrounded by palm trees. It looked like something off of a Sinbad movie, or something she expected to see near a beach in Miami.

She tried to focus on what she had to do. The gun she had seemed heavy and she had to make sure she had the safety off like Troy had told her.

When she was certain that she had it off, she slid along the wall to the code box for the security system. She checked it and found that it was off. She didn't even need the code!

Slowly she snuck up alongside the large glass doors that led into the kitchen area. She could see a side stairway that spiraled upward to the second level. She checked the sliding door and found it too was unlocked.

She slid the door open just enough to fit

through, then tip toed over to the other doorway.

She could hear a loud T.V. playing at the front of the house, so she followed the sound.

A few times she got lost in all the rooms. She kept having to back track until she found the dining room.

She stood looking into the living room when she realized that someone was sitting on the couch playing with the remote. The flat screen was massive and the person on the couch had their head down holding a huge remote control trying to figure out how it worked. As the female kept pushing buttons, the stereo system went on and off, then the television blinked on and off.

Smallworld snuck up behind them hoping they wouldn't look back as she approached. When she was right behind the woman sitting on the couch, Sunshine looked back behind her with a surprised look on her face as Smallworld pulled the trigger.

BOP! BOP! BOP! BOP! BOP! The gun went off in automatic modes as she held down the trigger. Brain matter and skull fragments covered the furniture like an abstract painting.

Where Sunshine's head had once been whole, there were a number of vacancies showing where the bullets tore chunks out of her skull. Smallworld threw up from the sight of the woman's ruined head. She just couldn't help it as her stomach heaved up it's contents.

When she was able to gather herself, she ran out of the room terrified and screaming as she cried from the guilt of what she'd done.

She was scared the woman was gonna get up like she'd seen in the zombie movies to chase her. In her mind the woman was right behind her covered in blood, with holes in her head. Her paranoia made her believe that if she looked back, the woman would be able to catch her. She never looked back.

When she got close to Troy's car she was afraid he wouldn't be there and started crying and moaning.

She ran faster and grabbed the door startling Troy who sat sleeping as he waited.

When she slammed into the door in a hurry to get in, Troy jumped and pulled the gun he had tucked under his arm as he napped.

"Bitch! I coulda killed you! Why you run all up on the car like dat?"

Smallworld just kept crying. It wasn't like Troy said it would be. She was scared and had killed two people. She didn't know how she was gonna sleep now.

Troy started his car and pulled from the back of the house in a hurry to get out of the complex. He drove with his lights out till he was well away from the front entrance. When they were out of the complex and on their way, he asked Smallworld what happened.

"Ain't nobody see you did they?" He asked as Smallworld just kept crying.

She sniffled, "No!"

"Den bitch, what you crying for?"

Smallworld huffed and tried to wipe the snot running down her nose, "I'm, I'm, I'm scared," she said between breaths.

Troy just shook his head disgusted. "You sure you got her? I don't want that bitch ta live through dis shit. Was she breathin?"

Smallworld tried to pull herself together because she could see that Troy was getting mad and that scared her almost as much as the vision of the woman's brains all over the room she'd just left. He had an evil look in his eyes that made him appear possessed.

"She wan' breathing! I'm sure!"

Troy nodded his approval. "Good! Now get yourself together girl! You makin me think you can't handle this shit! And what the fuck is that smell?!?"

Smallworld covered her mouth, embarrassed by the fact that she had thrown up.

"I can handle it!" She lied as she tried to put on a straight face.

"I don't want your ass gettin scared and tellin yo' Momma our business, understand? If you do, yo momma gon go ta jail too! Ya heard me?"

Smallworld just nodded her head as she looked over at Troy.

They drove until they got to the end of her block. Troy pulled over on the corner, dug in his pocket and gave Smallworld a coupla hundred dollars. He didn't even give her the money he promised, and Smallworld was in no mood to argue. She hurried up out of the car and snuck back into her room.

Troy drove back to his house whistling "Pop goes the Weasel."

****

Cam'ren pulled into his parents' home. He smiled fondly thinking about the memories he'd had in their home. He could only hope that they would be proud of him.

He was about to graduate from college "and" get married to the woman of his dreams.

Cam'ren stepped down out of his Denali truck and looked up to the front window.

His adopted mother usually stayed up waiting for his father to come home from a late shift. She could never sleep until she knew he'd made it home.

Cam'ren unlocked the door and stepped into the living room as his mother was coming down the steps in her night gown, assuming that he was his father Stephen.

"Had a rough????"

She stopped on the steps, "Cam'ren! What are you doing here! I thought you were your father!"

Cam'ren walked to meet her at the base of the steps. "I've got a surprise for you Mom! I'm getting married!"

Mary ran down the steps and jumped into Cam'ren's arms. "Congratulations I'm so proud of you!"

Cam'ren beamed at the affection from his mother.

He put her down after their hug, and heard the door shut behind them.

Stephen stood looking at the two of them with a worn and worried look on his face. He didn't seem at all pleased to see Cam'ren. He put down his keys as he greeted Cam'ren. "When did you get in town?"

"I just got here Pop! I wanted to surprise you!"

He looked at his wife wondering if she knew he was coming. The puzzled look on her face let him know that she didn't know.

Stephen was a detective by nature, he could read people's body language and always had a question about things if they didn't feel right. He was like a bloodhound, that's what made him good at his job.

The first day that he'd met Cam'ren's brother Cam'ron, he could see the young man was trouble.

When he started investigating Cam'ron's background further, he definitely didn't like what he saw.

Cam'ron was under investigation by the feds for money laundering, and drug trafficking. The only reason they hadn't been able to bust him is because of the front he used through his real estate business.

He wanted to tell Cam'ren these things, but

didn't want to make it seem like he was trying to come between him and his brother.

What was troubling him now was how he was going to tell Cam'ren that there had been a shooting at his brother's address. He was coming home to let his wife know first. He just couldn't tell her on the phone and have her worrying.

"Does your brother know you're coming?"

Cam'ren was puzzled at the sour expression on his father's face. "No, when I got there he'd just left town. Pop, what's the matter."

Stephen pulled his son into the living room and sat him down as Mary sat beside him. Stephen looked very serious and his expression made Mary start looking worried.

"Son, I don't know how to tell you this, but there was just a shooting call at your brother's house. I just came home to let your mother know what was going on before I head over to the scene."

Cam'ren looked horrified. "Are you sure it was the right address! There are a lot of houses on the property. It couldn't have been Cam'ron's house. I just left there."

"No son, I'm sure and I'm on my way over there to see what's going on."

Cam'ren jumped up, "Well I'm going with you!"

****

Stephen and Cam'ren pulled up to the gate of Cam'ron's estate in Cam'ren black Yukon.

They both could see police lights dancing off of the façade of Cam'ron's home as they looked down the Palm Tree lined driveway.

There was yellow crime scene tape everywhere. Sheriffs and detectives were roaming the property with flash lights.

"What the hell is going on here?" Cam'ren asked his father while looking at all the activity.

Whatever it is, it isn't good," answered Cam'ren's father as Cam'ren began rolling down the window when they pulled up to the house.

"Do either of you gentleman live at this address?" The officer asked as he flashed his flashlight into their faces.

"Jeff, it's me Stephen. What's going on up there?"

The sheriff shined the light over at Cam'ren's father, "Oh, hey Detective Jackson. I didn't know it was you. Are you investigating this case too?"

Stephen leaned over Cam'ren as he spoke, "No, this is something of a family matter for my son. Can you give me any information on what happened?"

Well sir, I can only give information to the family members." He said as he looked back down the driveway.

Cam'ren cut in, "This is my brother's place!"

The cop looked back to Cam'ren, "So where is your brother now?"

Cam'ren was getting pissed, no one was telling him what had happened, "I don't know sir.

I just got into town myself."

Stephen put his hand on his son's shoulder as he got the officer's attention back. "Jeff, we're gonna drive up. I'll see you later."

As a black detective, Stephen still had to deal with the racism of his white co-workers. He was a senior detective and the other white officers often felt he still wasn't equal to them, even with his rank.

"Alright, come on through," he said as he waved them through."

They drove through and parked in the drive way. They both got out of the car and Stephen asked Cam'ren to give him a minute while he tried to find out what had happened. Cam'ren kept looking at the people in front of the house hoping he'd see Sunshine.

As he stood waiting, he saw a car moving at a high rate of speed down the driveway. A number of officers had to jump out of the way as Pam hit the brakes. Dust and gravel went everywhere.

She came over and ran up to Cam'ren. "Cam'ren, what happened? What's going on?"

Cam'ren really didn't know and kept worrying about Sunshine.

"I don't know. I just got here with my father. He's checking with the other detectives to find out what happened."

Another detective came from around the back of the house with an evidence bag so Cam'ren approached him. "Excuse me detective, can you please tell me what's going on?"

The cop shook his head. "Sorry son, someone was murdered in this house. We only knew about it from an anonymous caller."

Just as the detective finished telling Cam'ren this, two men from the coroner's office came out carrying a body bag with Sunshine's body in it.

Cam'ren lost it......

CHAPTER 15

Cam'ron got a call on his cell right before pulling in to D.C. He checked to see who it was, and when he saw it was Pam, he let it go straight to voice mail.

He didn't want to argue with Pam, he had work to do. The bitch Nancy had to go and he was kicking himself in the ass for having even fucked with her to begin with.

Smash pulled off into Champ's Motel. They both had fake I.D. on them that they could use to register under an alias. Cam'ron and Smash both checked the names they would be using, and made sure that the credit cards were in the spare wallets they'd be using the entire time they were in D.C.

They pulled the guns and clothes out and stepped in to register. With that done, they put the guns in their room and met back at the truck.

Smash drove to a car rental spot back out on the highway. Cam'ron waited as Smash went in to get another car. When he came out, he followed Smash back to the motel.

When they got back in the room, they both got together in Cam'ron's room to talk

"My Dude, you gon have to get rid a ya boy Troy!" Smash said as Cam'ron laid on the bed to relax after the long drive.

Cam'ron looked at Smash as he smoked his Dutch in the chair across from the bed. He knew it was going to come down to having to choose between the two of them. He just didn't want to do it the way that it was going down.

Smash was his partner, but Troy had been with him since the beginning. He still owed him his loyalty.

"Why can't y'all jus squash that shit between y'all my dude? We all family, ain't we?"

Smash wasn't tryna hear that shit. "That niggah ain't family my dude. All he seem to care about is the connect. You too blind ta see. That niggah ain't really feelin you. Ya Heard?"

Cam'ren thought back to how their relationship had changed. He'd trusted Troy, but there was a lot he didn't know about him. He had too many secrets that when Cam'ron really started to look at, left him suspicious.

Troy hadn't been the same since he'd switched up his distribution and started working with Smash's people Drag and June.

Cam'ron had never asked how he got rid of the coke that he provided through his connect Tank, so long as the money was right on Troy's end, he saw no reason to. He just saw a better situation with Drag and June that felt safer.

When Cam'ron made that decision, Troy started changing. At first Cam'ron thought it was just because he felt out of the loop. Now he was suspecting that it could be more.

He thought back to how Troy kept trying to

get hooked up to deal with his connect Tank. He kept using the excuse that Cam'ron was too busy taking care of cleaning his money and didn't need to handle the product side of the business.

Cam'ron just wasn't sure. Troy could've just wanted a more active role in the organization and a chance to prove himself. Cam'ron didn't want to betray his friend over unproven suspicions.

Cam'ron had to be sure.

He looked back over at Smash, "We gon work that out later, right now we gotta get some sleep."

Smash let it go. "I feel you on that. I need a few hours myself since I had to keep my eyes on the road."

Cam'ron set his D&G watch to wake him at twelve Friday afternoon.

****

Cam'ren sat in the living room of his adopted parents' house exhausted both emotionally and physically.

He'd been to the morgue to identify Sunshine's body and still didn't know how to locate her next of kin. His father had a few friends working on that and sat across from him with Mary at his side to give Cam'ren support.

"I don't understand why this happened Pop! She doesn't even know anyone here that we know of. Why would somebody want to kill her?"

Stephen shook his head as if he was

struggling with something he wanted to say. When he finally found the words he was looking for, he let Cam'ren know what "he" knew. "Son, I don't think it was about your girlfriend. I think it was about your brother and the people he does business with."

Cam'ren recoiled from his father's words like he'd been slapped in the face.

"What the hell are you talking about Pop? My brother is a real estate developer. Why would anyone want to kill him?"

As he said the words out of his mouth, he knew how stupid he sounded. He knew the lifestyle that his brother lived growing up. He just didn't want to accept what he already knew. His brother was a criminal and powerful enough of a person to have enemies that wanted to kill him.

The cars, mansions, and even his truck were all the spoils of his illegal business. He wasn't an ordinary business man at all, he was a thug, a gangster, a drug kingpin, and a killer, and his father knew it!

Cam'ren got up off the couch trying to digest the reality of everything he'd experienced in the last few days.

His falling in love with two women that he hardly knew, and his finding a twin brother who he hardly knew made him feel naive and torn apart inside.

Stephen understood how he felt. He'd tried to protect Cam'ren from the type of people he ended up surrounding himself with, but in the end, Cam'ren had made his own choices. Now they were coming back to haunt him.

"Listen son, you have a chance at a wonderful future putting these type of people away. Your brother is a criminal who peddles death in our communities and this is the result of "his" choices.

"You've gotta accept that reality! It's a reality I've worked with as a detective for all these years. The kind of person that your brother is will only bring death in his wake. You need to see that or you'll end up a casualty just like your girlfriend."

Cam'ren didn't want to believe what his father was saying about his brother. It was like his father knew more than he was saying, "Your acting like my brother is already guilty in your mind! You don't even know him and you didn't know Sunshine, so how could you say that."

Stephen looked Cam'ren in the eyes and told him the truth of what he knew. "I know that girl you were gonna marry was a prostitute. She had a rap sheet for solicitation as long as my arm.

"I know your brother is one of the South's biggest drug traffickers and will be busted by the feds eventually. I also know that if you keep getting mixed up with that brother of yours, your gonna ruin your chances of working for the F.B.I.

"Then all the people that I've been talking to to get you in, so that you can put away those types of people you've been hanging around with, will be hunting you "and" your brother down. Do you understand that?"

There it was. Plain and simple. Cam'ren had to choose an oath that would lead to loyalty to his brother, or turning his back on the only real family that he had.

He had to choose.

****

"Suck it like you love it," Troy yelled at Smallworld as he forced her head up and down.

"Umm, ummm!" She moaned as he went in and out of her little mouth.

He slapped her, and when he did, she gagged as she fell back on her knees.

"Take them clothes off!" He ordered her as he rose up off of the motel room bed. When she was too slow, he slapped her again and started ripping her clothes off. Smallworld tried to scream and he covered her mouth as he continued to beat her.

"You dumb little bitch! You fucked up!"

It was all over the morning news. She hadn't killed Pam at all. She'd killed some other woman that Troy had never seen before in Cam'ron's house. His father was gonna be pissed!

He pulled his belt from around his and began beating the girl as he tied her up. He ripped every shred of clothes off of the little girl then picked her up and threw her on the bed.

Standing at the bed's edge looking down on

her he wanted to punish her by taking out all the rage he'd felt at everything that had happened in the last few days as he stroked himself.

He bent over and grabbed the grease off of the night stand table by the bed and began lubricating the full length of his erect penis. He reached up between Smallworld legs and lubricated her insides as she whimpered with her torn clothes stuffed in her mouth to muffle her screams.

He turned her over on her stomach positioning himself at the opening of her ass hole and rammed himself inside of her. Smallworld screamed in agony as flames shot through her bowels.

Troy didn't care, he just went deeper and deeper pumping with all his might to make sure that every thrust of his manhood caused her pain.

The tightness of her anal muscles wrapped around him like a vice causing him to explode inside of her within minutes after violating the young child.

Her screams aroused him, giving voice to his anger, so he did it to her again, and again, and again.

When he was done, he left her lying there soiled with blood and feces. He stepped into the small bathroom to clean himself up, then came back out into the room.

While he began to put his clothes back on his phone rang. He stepped into the bathroom to see who it was. Within minutes, he had his clothes on and was heading towards his father's house with Smallworld left in the room tied up.

****

Cam'ron's D&G watch went off at 12:00 exactly. He jumped out of bed as though he had a hot date.

He stepped next door to wake Smash up after he got dressed. Smash came to the door still half sleep as Cam'ron stepped in with the bag of guns.

"Yo my dude, you rolling out or what?"

"Yeah, yeah, I'm ready." Smash answered half sleep with a Dutch hanging off of his lips.

"Come on then. I'm tryna do this and get the hell out of here!"

Smash tried to wipe the cold out of his eyes. "Damn niggah, let me hit my gums!"

He closed the door behind Cam'ron as Cam'ron took a seat to wait. He dug into the bag of guns and put a .44 Bull Dog, a .357. Magnum, and a knife on the bed as Smash made his way to the bathroom.

As Smash went by, he looked on anticipation of holding the .357 and the knife.

Cam'ron knew exactly what Smash's weapons of choice were.

Within minutes, Smash was out of the bathroom and tucking his two weapons. "Come on, I'm ready my dude." He said heading for the door.

"Here," Camron said while tossing him the rental car keys.

They jumped into the rental and made their way to Nancy's house.

Cam'ron pulled out his phone and dialed Nancy's number.

"Hello!" She said like she was out of breath from working out or something.

"Hey Baby, where you at?" Cam'ron asked, smiling on the other end.

"Oh, I'm in the condo. I just got back from working out in the gym downstairs."

"So you're in the house?" Cam'ron asked nonchalantly.

Nancy started getting suspicious.

"Why are you asking me where I am? Are you getting jealous? You didn't even want to talk to me yesterday."

"Well I missed you baby, and I wanted to know what you are doing." Cam'ron lied.

"I plan on staying in most of the day. I still have a few more resumes I have to send out. So I'll try to get those out."

"Well don't be shocked if you get a surprise visit!"

Nancy started laughing, "Ooh! You bad boy, you know how I love surprises," she said lustfully.

"Yeah! And this is gonna be the best surprise yet!" Cam'ron said trying to get her horny.

Nancy giggled seductively again before she answered, "I hope you give it to me soon. You makin me wet just waitin on you."

Cam'ron could tell by her voice she was probably finger popping herself on the phone in anticipation. Nancy was just a freak like that and he used it to his advantage.

"I should be there soon. Just leave the door open for me. I'll see you at eight." Then he hung up before she could ask anymore questions.

****

"How the fuck did yo' people fuck up and just kill that girl? What kinda people you hirin man?" Barked Mickey.

"Come on Pop! I put my people on it! They just fucked up. I'ma make this shit right." Troy pleaded with his father.

"Yeah, and look what your people did out there. You done made a damn mess!" He shot back at Troy.

"Don't worry, I'll punish my people fo' their mistake!" He promised his father.

"Get the hell out of my damn house and don't come back till you handle yo' business! I don't even wanna look at ya! You makin me sick!"

Aloe came in to see what all the yelling was about. Mickey nodded to her for her to show Troy the door. Aloe looked at Troy with sympathy. She didn't say anything since Mickey was her first love.

That she loved Troy's young ass was a secret that she could never let Mickey know. If he ever found out, Aloe would've been dead and in the Santee River. Something she tried to put off for as long as possible.

On her way out she turned to Mickey, "Do you need me to take care of anything?"

"I need you to run up to the Piggly Wiggly and get me some of that pork bacon that's on sale!" He said trying to get her out of the house. He looked impatient so Aloe left without comment.

Mickey hollered for Tyson to step into his office. Tyson had been Mickey's bodyguard and lover for years.

What very few people knew was that Mickey was a closet faggot. He'd started dipping into the dookie jar while he was in the feds.
Tyson came in to see what Mickey wanted.

"We gotta hurry up befo' that bitch come her stinkin ass back!" Tyson moved over to the back of the desk where Mickey sat reclining and started pulling his pants down. He bent over Mickey's desk and started teasing him with his ass in the air.

Mickey always liked to have sex when he was stressed. Tyson was always there to accommodate him with what he liked.

Mickey started stroking himself after pulling down his pants, then spit in his hand, rubbed it on himself, and started wearing Tyson's well-muscled ass out.

"Fuck me harder Daddy!" Moaned Tyson while grabbing the edge of Mickey's desk. He howled like a cold bitch as Mickey pounded him from behind.

Just as they were finishing their down low trist, they both panicked as they heard someone come in the front door.

Mickey quickly pulled himself out of Tyson's rectum and tried to hurry up and fix his clothes.

Tyson hauled his big ass out of Mickey's office and up the stairs.

As Summer walked in the front door, the foul smell of shit wafted up and hit her in the nose. She crinkled her face in disgust, "Ooh! What the hell is that smell?" She asked while fanning her face.

Mickey walked out of the back office and down the hall to meet her as Tyson snuck up the back stairs.

"I ain't smelled nothin until you walked yo' funky ass up in here like yo' motherfuckin ass pay rent or something!" Mickey shot at her by way of greeting.

Summer looked irritated and in no mood for Mickey's remarks. "Well ya ass don't say that when you need me to come over here and cook and clean for yo' ass, and suck that little wrinkled up dick of yours!"

Mickey just ignored her. "What yo' ass want anyway? I ain't in a good mood!"

Summer perked right up considering the argument over. "I thought Aloe was over here?"

"She was, but I sent her out to get me some pork bacon they got at the Piggly Wiggly."

He could tell Summer wanted something. She wasn't her usual cantankerous self.

"Well I need a few bucks, so that I can buy something to wear to the club!" Stated Summer absently as she placed her keys in her small Coach bag.

Mickey huffed, "What yo ass need to do is get a motheruckin job!" He was still mad that Summer had messed up his chocolate train ride.

"I do have a job, takin care a yo' ass. It ain't my fault you ain't had nothin for us to do!"

Mickey smiled sheepishly as a plan developed in his mind.

"You still got a feeler out on that boy Cam'ron?"

"I been waitin for him to call me, but I can probably get close if I'm in the right place. Why? What you up to?"

Mickey just smiled as a plan started formulating in his mind.

****

At 8:00 p.m. Cam'ron and Smash rode up on the elevator that led to Nancy's condo. The place was nice, but Cam'ron wasn't there to enjoy the scenery.

They stepped off of the elevator and rang Nancy's door bell.

She came to the door in a black Victoria's

Secret negligee ensemble with her hair cascading down around her shoulders. She held a drink in her hands as she cocked her hip to one side in a pair of high heeled stilettos.

"Hey baby!" Cam'ron said from the doorway.

Nancy's eyes lit up in anticipation when she saw Smash. She'd hoped it was a chance for round two of the Ménage.

"I told you I was gonna surprise you," Cam'ron said as he stepped in and started fondling her breast. Nancy moaned in anticipation as she back pedaled away from the door.

Smash stepped in right behind them and closed the door as he removed his jacket.

Cam'ron scooped Nancy up off the floor and carried her into the bedroom as Smash stayed right on his heels.

Nancy looked at Cam'ron dreamy eyed, then kissed him like a long lost lover.

"See, I knew you'd be back," she whispered as he laid her on the bed.

Cam'ron stood back to take a look at her as Smash moved to the other side of the bed with his hand behind his back.

"Are you ready for your surprise now Nancy?" He asked with a devilish grin on his face.

Nancy arched her back like a horny cat then nodded in expectation.

Cam'ron looked at Smash, Smash shrugged, then pulled a large army knife from behind his back and stabbed down into Nancy's throat.

He caught her dead center, cutting off all chances of letting her scream, then began drawing the knife across her throat.

Nancy's face was frozen in shock as she kicked and tried to gasp for air.

Cam'ron grabbed her arms as she tried to reach up and grab Smash's hands. Within minutes, she released her bowels as Smash practically cut Nancy's head off.

When Smash was done, Cam'ron and Smash flipped the house to make it look like a robbery, wiped down the front door, cleaned the blood off of themselves, then got into the rental to go back to their motel.

On the way, Cam'ron checked his telephone and saw that there was more than one message for him from Pam.

He called Pam at the house and got no answer, so he checked his other messages.

Noticing a message from his brother, he called him.

When Cam'ron answered, that is when all hell broke loose!

CHAPTER 16

Smallworld lay tied up in the bed for hours crying and uncertain if Troy intended to come back and kill her. She struggled against the rags that Troy had made to tie her up from her clothes.

When she had to go to the bathroom, the pain of holding it after being abused the way that she was gave her the courage to try and untie her hands.

She didn't know how long she struggled to free her hands, but when she was finally able to get loose, it was dark outside.

She rolled over to look around the room and noticed that the door was ajar. A shadow stood in the door and she was afraid that Troy had been standing there waiting to see if she broke free, just so he could kill her.

She ran into the bathroom and slammed the door while she looked frantically around the room for a place to hide.

Someone knocked on the bathroom door and started asking her if she was alright. She didn't recognize the voice as belonging to Troy, so she gave the person on the other side of the door a piece of her young mind.

She waited listening as she heard footsteps

leaving, then heard the front door close to the room she was in. When she thought it was safe, she stepped into the room shivering from fear and the cold in the room.

A shadow moved to her right, and, as she ducked to get away from the pale figure attempting to grab her, she realized that the old white man in her room had no clothes on.

She jumped over the bed and looked at the old man as he blocked the door to keep her from getting out of the room.

"Get yo' pale white ass out of my room befo' I call the police!" She barked at the man.

The man laughed at her like a mad villain off of the cartoons she used to watch.

"They'd love to hear how you were up in here prostituting!" He shot back with a wicked grin.

"Yo ass is crazy, dat was my Daddy!" She lied, trying to convince herself that the white man in her room might believe her.

The old white man looked at her with the "Come on" look, as he inched a little closer.

"So you and yo' daddy have intercourse?" He whispered as he started fondling his little private parts in front of her.

Smallworld was really scared now. The man in her room wasn't sane and he was moving closer to her inch by inch.

"I don't know what your crazy ass is talkin," about she yelled, then tried to jump back across the bed and into the bathroom.

The white man moved with the speed of a track star and grabbed her as she tried to make it over the bed.

"Get yo' nasty hands off me!" She screamed as she kicked and punched. He wrestled with her until he was able to climb on top of her and put a hand over her mouth.

Smallworld could feel the vomit rising up in her throat from the rancid smell that came off of the man's hands and body.

The man reached down between her legs and spread them so wide it hurt. He straddled her with his own legs and jammed himself inside of her.

She tried to scream again as the man forced his way up into her uterus with reckless abandon. He pumped harder and faster the more that she tried to scream, as if her agony excited him even more.

Smallworld bit down on his hand until she tasted blood and the man screamed, "Ooh! You little black bitch!"

He punched her over and over again until Smallworld lost consciousness from all the blows to her head.

When Smallworld woke up, it was morning, and every inch of her cried out with agony. She tried to swallow and tasted blood that sat caked on her tongue like tar.

The crazed man that had beaten and raped her lay snoring next to her and when she tried to get up he opened his eyes to look her dead in her face.

Smallworld screamed and tried to crawl away from the maniacal stare of the old man as he lay casually like her long lost lover.

"Hey Sunflower! Good morning! Are ya hungry?" He asked as if he'd never violated and beat her the night before.

She could see that he really wasn't in the room or didn't really see who she actually was. The man was having delusions of another person in a past life.

Smallworld wasn't sure if she would live through the ordeal she'd experienced in the last 24 hours. It was just too much for her young mind to deal with. She began praying like never before for the nightmare that she was living through to end. She asked God to please take her as quickly as possible so that she wouldn't have to feel anymore pain.

Just as she finished her last words of supplication, Troy stepped into the room.

The look of bewilderment and rage she saw written on Troy's face made her run and hide in a corner. He looked at the man lying on the bed, then without one word, he reached into the small of his back and pulled out a .40 caliber. He pulled the trigger and the bullet pierced the man's chest sending the man sprawling across the bed.

Troy rushed over and grabbed Smallworld, pulled her into the bathroom and wrapped her in a towel. He carried her out of the room and down to his waiting car.

He drove her back to a small trailer he used from time to time to bag up his personal product.

He laid Smallworld down on the old rickety couch he had in the living room, then went to the back to find something for her to wear.

He found an old grey sweat suit he thought would fit her and threw it to her while she lay huddled on the couch.

"Clean yo' self-up! I'ma take you home. Hurry up cause your Momma will be coming home from the hospital today!"

Smallworld limped into the bathroom and closed the door. She used an old soiled hand towel to wash herself as best she could, then she put the sweat suit on over her bruised and battered body. When she was done, she came out to find Troy sitting there waiting for her.

He had a very serious look on his face and she hoped that he wasn't about to kill her. He looked up at her with a distant look in his eyes.

"I don't ever want you to talk about what just happened to anybody. You done already fucked up to where I should just kill yo' ass. I just don't wanna hear yo' Momma's mouth. If anybody asked, you got jumped for what happened at the game, unda' stand?"

Smallworld nodded and went to sit on the couch until Troy was done making a few calls. When he was done, he motioned her to leave and they both got into the car.

Moments later they pulled into the driveway of her mother's trailer. Tamara and Rita both limped out covered in bandages to greet them. When they saw Smallworld's condition they both looked very worried.

Troy rolled down his driver side window, "Look, don't give her a hard time. She's been through enough in the last few days."

Tamara looked like she was ready to give him some lip, but thought better of it.

Since Tamara didn't wanna push the issue with Troy in the condition she was in, she took it out on Smallworld.

"Get yo' ass up in that house!" She looked over at Rita who was watching Troy with hawk eyes as he drove off, then they both followed Smallworld into the house.

****

Troy drove over to the stash house. It was time to get payback for all of the shit that he'd had to put up with just to get at Cam'ron's connect. If he couldn't get the connect from Cam'ron outright, he decided it was time to just cut his losses and take the product and the money Cam'ron kept at the stash.

With that gone, Cam'ron would eventually have to go back to his connect to re-up or he wouldn't be able to make his drops with his distributors. He'd follow him and eventually find out who his connect was so that he could kill him and set up his own distribution.

When he got to the stash house, Shamrock

answered the door nodding his head to the reggae rhythm pulsing through a small radio in the kitchen.

"Big up Troy! Where ya been! Cam'ron's been trying to call you!"

"When did he call? My phones been fucked up."

"Said he was on his way back in. He should be back already."

As Shamrock turned around from locking the door, Troy pulled the trigger on the .40 cal he pulled from his waist as Shamrock had his back to him.

BLAM! BLAM! BLAM!

The shot's rang out hitting Shamrock in his upper torso. His body jerked frantically then slid down the door as his head slumped over to the side.

Troy dragged him up off the door then signaled to the squad of young bucks he had waiting up the street in the car.

Two young men jogged up with trash bags in hand ready to load up as another one backed the car down into the stash spots driveway.

Troy led the three young men to the back porch, then started to move the chest freezer out from against the back wall.

He pulled the trap door that the freezer covered and hit the light switch as he moved down the steps.

Cocaine stood on elevated palettes in stacks 10 high! The men moved quickly loading up bag's in a chain gang line as one filled then handed the bricks over to the next person until every palette was empty. While they loaded all the bricks into the bags, Troy walked over to a small antique bank safe and began unloading all the money they had stashed to re up on product.

Within twenty minutes the men had all of the product loaded up into the vehicle and were driving back to the old trailer that Troy had just taken Smallworld to.

When everything was safely stowed and accounted for, he set up a guard around the perimeter of the trailer and made a call.

"Pop? Yeah, it's me. I'm good on my end. Go head and make yo' move tonight."

Mickey hung up on the other end, turned to Summer and Aloe and said, "Time to make gangster moves ladies. Handle yo' business."

****

CHAPTER 17

"Brothers and sisters, we are gathered here today to lay to rest a child of God! A sister who was loving to those who knew her, and kind even to those she didn't know. Now I know that many of you here only got to know this young sister momentarily, but in that time she was able to touch each of you who are seated here on her behalf.

"Her momentary time among each of you is an analogy of each of our lives, for we each have only a brief moment in this world before we may be called back to the Heavenly Father!"

Cam'ren sat listening to the eulogy of Sunshine. His mother and father sat on either side of him, comforting him as he said his farewells to the woman he'd planned to marry.

Cam'ren had not said much since the talk he had with his father, and as he looked at the woman that he loved so dearly, he thought back to the funeral of his mother. He was sitting in the place of his father and could understand how his father felt when his mother passed.

As the minister continued in his eulogy of Sunshine, he paused momentarily as Cam'ron walked in with his partner, and two elderly gentlemen leaning heavily on canes as they walked.

Pam sat two rows back veiled in black, sobbing occasionally before turning to see who walked in to attend the funeral. Her surprise was veiled behind the lace of her designer black hat.

She hadn't seen Cam'ron since he'd left her the night that Sunshine died, and the anticipation of talking to him quelled the sorrow she felt for Cam'ren's future fiancé.

Cam'ren nodded to his brother as he walked up to the casket and kissed Sunshine's hand, then said a prayer for her. When he was done, he turned to his brother and gave him a nod of condolence before taking his seat beside Pam just two rows back.

The two elderly gentlemen that accompanied Cam'ron took a seat in the last pew, while Smash stepped forward and said his farewells to Sunshine before sitting directly behind Cam'ron.

Cam'ren could feel the irritation in his father's demeanor and tried his best to ignore it for the sake of Sunshine.

When the final words were said, Cam'ren Cam'ron, Dutch, Cam'ren's Father Stephen, and the two elderly men all carried Sunshine's body out of the church and into the waiting stretch Cadillac that would convey Sunshine's body to her resting place.

****

Aloe and Summer sat watching the entire funeral procession. They expected Cam'ron to show his face at the funeral, but to have him show up with their two targets was a plus that neither Summer or Aloe anticipated.

Each of them readied the Uzzi sub-machine guns they tucked under their trench coats, then continued loading spare magazines with bullets.

When all was ready they would strike and take out all opposition to Mickey's organization in one fell swoop.

They followed the family to the grave site and parked a good distance from where Sunshine's body would be laid to rest. Each got out and stretched against the snugness of the black leotard body suits they had on.

They tied black bandanas around their faces to cover their identities, then began moving like black panthers through the rows of tombstones.

At a good clip from where the final words were said over Sunshine's grave site, they each split up to flank the family members as they stood saying their farewells. Cam'ren wept considerably as he saw the casket of his beloved about to be lowered into it's final destination.

As he turned away and wept on his mother's shoulder, he never saw death coming for him and everyone he loved.

Aloe stepped up from behind a large tombstone and unleashed a controlled burst of fire in the direction of the entire procession of the onlookers.

BRRRRRRRRRRRIIP!
BRRRRRRRRRRRRRRRRRIP

Hearing Aloe's repeat fire spraying to the left, Summer rose from an obelisk like commemorative stone topped with the Arch Angel Michael, and began to cut on the opposite side.

BRRRRRRRRRRRRRRRRRRRRRIP!
BRRRRRIIPPPP!

The family was pinned. The two elderly gentlemen took to the cover of the folding chairs with surprising agility as they reached into their coats.

Bullets riddled the minister as his life's blood splattered the pages of his Holy Bible.

Stephen dove covering his wife as he pulled his field issued 9 millimeter.

Cam'ren looked back to see Cam'ron moving to his left to take cover by the coffin as he drew his own .40 caliber so Cam'ren followed him forward for cover.

When they were along the side of the coffin, another volley of flowers and wood sprayed as their attackers fired in the area where each of them had just stood.

A loud BOOM! BOOM! BOOM! Was fired from behind the two brothers as they looked back to see Stephen placing well aimed shots in the direction of the bullets to their right.

Cam'ron looked back and started inching to the left with gun in hand.

Summer ducked as chunks of concrete from return fire danced across the stone cover she'd chosen. Neither of them expected there to be much resistance or return fire, and weren't as close as they should have been to adequately use their weapons.

She looked to a tombstone further ahead of her that could give her a better shot, sprayed a burst of suppression fire, BRRIIIIIP!, then advanced closer to her targets. As she ran she pulled her spare clip.

Cam'ron peaked by the lower portion of the casket trying to get a head on the person who'd fired from his side. He saw footsteps and took aim. BOP! BOP! BOP! BOP! Down low bullets roared, and clipped the foot of the runner.

Stephen began climbing commando style forward in order to get a view between the tombstones where he'd just heard fire on his side. Seeing no one, he inched forward to the cover of an adjacent tombstone.

Mary looked horrified as he glanced back momentarily. She raised her hand pleadingly before a rapid succession of shots rang out behind Stephen.

BRRRRRRRRRRP BRRRRRRPI BRIIIIIIIIIP!

Mary was torn to pieces. Cam'ren and Stephen froze in horror as they both glanced behind them to see the bullets cut a path through her prone torso.

Pam screamed back behind the chair, as Mary's body danced as if it were electrocuted.

Within seconds, Drag and June were firing off successive shots in the direction of where the bullets had just been fired.

BOP! BOP! BOP! BOP! BOP! BOP! BOP! BOP!

Summer had moved during the distraction of the secondary volley to get a better shot and had only been able to hit the white woman.

In her haste to get a clear shot she gave up her cover and took two 357 Magnum slugs to her upper chest.

Her finger locked on the trigger of the small machine gun as her body was flung back with the momentum of each shot.

She died before she hit the ground.

Cam'ron and Cam'ren moved forward when a female cried as footsteps receded from their position. Cam'ron took his well-placed shots at the assailant on their side as they tried to retreat from the gun fight.

Seeing no more fire coming in their direction, they both moved forward, stooped, and low to the ground, as they moved from tombstone to tombstone, with Cam'ron leading. 40 yards out they found a large trail of blood and an empty magazine where their assailant had opened fire.

The twins scanned cautiously looking for the assailant and quickly spotted a fluttering trench coat moving among the monuments to the dead.

They both took off to give chase, and just as Summer rounded the bend in the road to get back to her vehicle, a click behind her made her turn, and take aim as she went.

Seeing Cam'ron's partner Smash with the drop on her, she froze.

Smash stood with his signature Dutch hanging from his lips as he dared the bitch to try pulling the trigger.

Cam'ron and Cam'ren arrived seconds later as Smash unarmed Aloe and pistol whipped her for good measure.

Both twins looked at the woman bleeding and unconscious before them on the ground. Recognition finally hit Cam'ron and Cam'ren. This was the bitch that Cam'ron had met on the side of the road "AND" the bitch who'd killed their father P-Love.

Rage welled up inside of each of them as they began to stomp the woman before Smash could intercede. It took a moment for both men to regain their composure.

Cam'ron immediately helped Smash get her into the trunk of the car after taking the keys she had in her trench coat pocket.

"I'ma take dis bitch to the spot my dude! I'll keep her tight til you get there."

Cam'ren motioned to Cam'ron, then ran back to the graveside to see who else had been injured.

When they got back they found Stephen weeping over his dead wife.

Cam'ron looked to his brother, "Cam'ren we gotta get outta here!"

Stephen looked up enraged, "Ain't nobody goin anywhere. You're all under arrest."

As he began to reach for his gun Cam'ren dove to try and grab it first. The two men struggled. Father and son tussled for a moment until, BOOOOM!

The gun went off.

****

Mickey sat waiting for a call to find out whether the hit on Drag and June had been a success. His irritability was always a sign to Tyson that Mickey was also horny.

He slid over beside Mickey on the side of the couch and put his head on his shoulder as he rubbed along Mickey's leg.

The two had been secret lovers for years. When Tyson had first begun working for Mickey he kept it to himself that his big ass was a faggot.

Eventually he'd been able to read the signs as word got back from the feds through mutual acquaintances that Mickey was also Bi-Sexual.

The two of them had lived a secret life with Tyson right there for him, even when he did more time in the feds.

What neither of them knew was that Mickey had contracted HIV during his last stent in the penitentiary.

He'd been out for nearly a year and a half and had infected everyone he'd had intercourse with. Summer, Aloe, Tyson, and Troy were each carriers of the deadly virus.

What Pam didn't know was that she too would be a casualty of Mickey's promiscuity.

The troubling thing was that Mickey knew he was HIV positive and didn't care. He just wanted his son to have a future before he died.

He loved Troy and felt guilty that for so many years he'd kept him as a secret from everyone but those closest to him.

This destroyed Troy and made him a cold blooded bastard just like his father.

What Troy didn't know was that "his" downfall was fast approaching. He had HIV from sleeping with his father's mistress and had the twins to deal with.

****

Rita walked into Smallworld's room and looked at her. Her mother Tamara had been sleeping throughout the day trying to recuperate from the injuries she'd sustained from the incident with Big Ruby. It pained her that the girl wasn't being cared for properly.

Smallworld lay with her head buried in the covers shivering as if she were sick.

Rita walked over and felt her forehead with her good hand, "Girl, what's wrong with you?"

Smallworld cringed, then began throwing up in the trashcan beside her bed.

Rita pulled back the covers as she tried to help Smallworld. When she did, she saw the bruises she'd acquired from her ordeal with Troy and the crazy white man who'd raped her after him.

Rita stood up shocked, "Girl, what happened to you?"

Smallworld began crying as she tried to cover herself. Rita wasn't having it. She quickly wrapped Smallworld in her blanket and started marching her to the car. As she went rushing out of the house she hollered to Tamara who was in her room convalescing, "Tamara I'll be back! I'm takin Smallworld to the doctor. She's sick!"

Tamara didn't even bother to move. She lay in a drunken stupor, high off of pain killers, and rum.

When Rita got no answer, she helped Smallworld to the car.

They drove to the emergency room and waited patiently for the doctor to see them.

CHAPTER 18

Cam'ron reached down and pulled his brother from the body of his father. As he did, he looked to each of them seeing blood stains covering both of their shirts.

"Cam'ren, are yo aiight bro! Cam'ren, answer me!"

Cam'ren looked up at his brother with an expression of shock and horror in his eyes. He looked back down at his adopted father's vacant eyes which stared accusingly back at him.

"Oh my God! Dad, please don't be dead! Dad, come on man get up! I'm sorry!" He pleaded as his father lay motionless in a pool of blood. He looked over at his adopted mother's lifeless body and wept uncontrollably until sirens could be heard in the distance.

Cam'ron grabbed the gun from his brother as June and Drag moved to quickly evacuate the premises.

"Young Buck! We gotta roll man. Five-O will be here in a minute! What you gonna do?"

Cam'ron threw the gun to Drag who quickly tucked the gun into his pocket like a hot potatoe. "Take my brother! I'ma stay here! Take him to your spot in the woods. I'll get at you when I can!" Cam'ron replied to the two elderly men.

June and Drag moved to grab Cam'ren under the arm and lead him off as quickly as their aged legs would permit. Cam'ron began developing a plan in his mind to explain what had just happened at Sunshine's funeral. He called back and handed Cam'ren his gun before watching as the two men hustled him into the car like a zombie.

The police arrived in minutes at the macabre scene splayed out across the lawn of the graveyard. Cam'ron stood stoicly pretending to weep as he himself issued another call to 911's emergency line to cover his failure to report the murders.

When the police arrived they fanned out with weapons drawn and ordered him to hit the ground.

"They killed my mother and father! They wrestled with him and took one of his weapons. He got one before they got away!" He lied as the officers began to question him.

As word went out that an officer had been killed, numerous spare officers and detectives converged on the scene. Many called him by his brother's name as if they were familiar with who he was. They believed him to be his brother and he never bothered to tell them the truth of the matter.

He was taken to the station where he was made to recount his version of events. An all-points bulletin was put out for Aloe according to the description that Cam'ron had given of her. He never bothered to tell the police that he knew exactly where she was until he made it safely away from the scene and was laying low.

He called Troy to give him the news.

****

Smallworld sat for hours in the hospital before she was finally seen. The hospital seemed to be in turmoil over the fact that a local cop had gotten killed from what Rita was able to gather.

When she was finally taken into a small cubicle partitioned by a long curtain for privacy, the doctors told her to wait patiently as they examined the young girl.

She waited for about twenty minutes as nurses moved back and forth from behind the curtain with all manner of medical apparatuses and needles. When the doctor was done treating Smallworld, the doctor came from behind the curtain with a somber look on his face.

"Ma'am, are you the one who escorted the young lady to the hospital?" He asked in his nasal and disjointed voice.

"Yes, that's my niece! What's wrong with her?"

The doctor did not look pleased. "I believe this child has been raped and beaten. She's experienced both vaginal and anal tearing and is suffering from some type of an infection. We're running some tests to see what the problem is, but we're gonna have to contact Social Services regarding the rape and assault."

Rita was shocked. She'd been hospitalized with her sister and had anticipated that Troy would've taken care of her niece for her sister. Now she was seeing that his claims of her being beaten by some of the girls who were close to Ruby was a lie. He'd assaulted her young niece and raped her to boot.

"Can I see her doctor?" She asked worried that she would be taken before she could confirm her suspicions.

"I'll allow a few moments with her before Child Services gets here, but I'm going to ask that you don't upset her anymore than she already is. I've given her a sedative to relax her. She may not be as coherent as you'd expect."

With that said, the doctor stepped to the side as Rita went into the cubicle where Smallworld lay with tubes in her arms.

Rita's eyes filled with tears as she looked at the sorry state of her young niece. She moved to her bed side and took her hand to console her.

"Smallworld Baby, can you hear me?"

Smallworld nodded as she looked up to the ceiling with a blank stare.

"Baby, I'm sorry! I didn't know someone had done this to you, but you gotta tell me the truth okay?"

Smallworld nodded. "Was it Troy that did this to you while we were in the hospital?"

Smallworld began to cry and turn away afraid to tell her aunt the truth. Her aunt wouldn't let her turn away completely and begged Smallworld to tell her the truth.

With a great sob Smallworld confessed to her aunt everything that Troy had done to her and made her do. When she was done telling her how he'd made her kill a person in a large mansion in a Good Real Estate complex, Rita knew that Troy had not only raped her niece, he'd allowed some sick old white man to violate her, and used her to try and kill Cam'ron.

As the doctor came in to usher her out of the cubicle, the desire for vengeance simmered in Rita's eyes. A desire that would also contribute to Troy's downfall.

****

The police didn't release Cam'ron until late in middle of the night. As soon as he stepped out of the station and got a good distance away, he placed a call to the pickup spot where Drag and June did their business.

"I'm out! Everything is covered and Cam'ron should be in the clear from what I told them. How's he doin?"

Drag looked back at Cam'ren who lay sleeping on the couch before responding,
"Your brother is fucked up man! He ain't said shit since we left the grave site. You need to get over here"

Cam'ron could understand, and his heart went out to his brother, but first he had to check to see if anyone else had been hit. He'd already gotten word that homicide had been to the stash spot and found Shamrock. He'd spent the last few days trying to get Intel on who could've possibly wanted to hit him. The streets weren't talking, and even Drag and June couldn't figure out who was trying to take him out.

Troy was nowhere to be found and hadn't answered his phone. He had no clue if he was dead or not, and assumed that he'd been hit by whoever was trying to kill him.

He turned his attention back to Drag who sat waiting on a response as to what he was gonna do.

"Listen, I'ma have Smash bring that bitch over to your place so we can interrogate her ass. We gonna get to the bottom of this! I'll be there in about an hour."

Cam'ron hung up the phone and called Pam. "Hey baby, are you alright?"

Pam began crying in the phone she was so happy to hear his voice. A million questions ran through her mind as she feared for the man she loved.

When she calmed down enough to listen to Cam'ron, he instructed her to get herself together and to go into hiding with her mother at a hotel out of town until he could figure out what was going on.

Pam begged to see him before she went, fearing that she would never see him again. Cam'ron had business to take care of. Love had to wait. This was the life that was chosen for him....

****

Rita drove back to the house that her and Tamara shared. When she walked in she found that Tamara was still asleep. She kicked open Tamara's door as Tamara jumped up startled out of her drunkin stupor.

"What the hell is wrong wit you Rita! You done lost your mind?" She screamed in anger at her sister.

Rita took three steps to Tamara's bed side and slapped her with a vicious back hand.

"You stupid bitch! You let that motherfucker up in this house. He raped my niece! He had her kill somebody, and now they gonna take her away because you brought that stinkin niggah up in here!"

Tamara lay clutching the side of her face and trying to grasp what her sister was saying through the fog of pills and alcohol.

"What the hell are you talkin about Rita?"

"Where's Smallworld?"

Rita began raining blows down on Tamara. "They took her you stupid bitch! They took her because Troy raped her and beat her! They gonna take your child because of that stupid bastard!"

As realization dawned on Tamara of just what Rita was saying, she began to weep. "Noo! I didn't know! They can't take my baby!"

Rita grabbed the phone, "You gotta call that motherfucker. Find out where he's at so we can get his ass! Call him!" She yelled as she shoved the phone at her sister.

Tamara dialed with shakey hands as she waited for Troy to respond.

"Hello," came an answer on the other and after only two rings.

"Troy, I need to see you! Smallworld is in the hospital! I need you to come here and take me to the hospital!"

Troy's face balled up on the other end of the phone. "Why you call me? Drive yo' ass over there then? You got a car!"

Tamara thought quickly, "I can't. My sister not here. I need you. They say she's real sick!"

Troy's lips smacked, "Listen, I can't come over now, so I'ma send somebody to take you to the hospital. They'll be there in about 45 minutes. You gonna be alright til then?"

"Yeah! Just hurry up! She's real sick and I need to get there as soon as I can."

Troy hung up and ordered his young buck Tyron to take the car and go to Tamara's house to take her to the hospital. The young buck moved out without any questions and within minutes was driving away from Troy's trailer.

As soon as Tamara hung up, Rita had Tamara call Pam's mother's number. Pam picked up on the second ring.

"Hello? Pam, this is Rita, Tamara's sister." They'd met a number of times previously and were on very good speaking terms since Troy and Cam'ron were so close.

What she told Pam would shock her to her core and give her answers that she knew Cam'ron would want to hear.

****

CHAPTER 19

Cam'ron stood waiting for a cab to pick him up when his phone rang. It was Pam again and she was sending a 911 message. He answered thinking that she wanted to complain about having to go into hiding.

"Hello?"

"Cam'ron, it's me Pam. Listen, Rita and Tamara just called me and told me that Troy is the one who had Sunshine killed. He was tryna kill me!"

"Why would he do that?" Cam'ron asked not really understanding Troy's motives.

Pam lied, "Probably to hurt you. But that's not what's important! He's been trying to get you all along! They don't know where he is, but one of his workers is on his way to pick Tamara up. He just left where ever Troy is!"

Just as she said this, Cam'ron's cab pulled up. He was only about 15 minutes away from Tamara and Rita's house. He asked Pam to hold on as he stepped into the cab and gave him directions to Tamara and Rita's house.

On the drive over, Pam gave him all the information that Rita had given her about Troy's having raped Smallworld and having forced her to try and kill Pam. When she was done running it all down to Cam'ron, he was just minutes away from Tamara and Rita's house.

Before hanging up, Pam begged him to be careful and told him she loved him, but Cam'ron had death on his mind.

The car pulled into the driveway and he paid the driver. Cam'ron stepped over to the house and realized that he didn't have a gun. He didn't know if the young buck that was coming to pick up Tamara was strapped, so he knew he had to be cautious in how he planned his next moves. This could be a set up planned by Troy to catch him off guard.

He knocked on the door and waited while checking behind him to make sure no one was laying in wait for him. Rita opened the door and stepped to the side to let him in.

Tamara sat on the couch bandaged about her head with two swollen eyes and a busted lip. Cam'ron cringed at the sight of her.

Rita had her one hand in a cast and had a number of bruises covering her face as well.

"I got word from Pam about what happened. Don't worry, I'ma handle that snake ass niggah, ya heard?"

Tamara nodded and hung her head in shame. Troy was supposed to be her man, and instead he'd used her and violated her child. She sat looking like a broken woman and Cam'ron didn't have the time to pity her. He needed a strap.

"Y'all got a gun in here?"

Rita pulled a snub nosed .38 from her waist. "This is all we got in here."

Cam'ron took the gun and checked it, then looked at both of the women, "Tamara, you stay here and answer the door. Rita, move your car and come back. I'm gonna need your ride. Aiight?"

Both women nodded agreement. Cam'ron took a deep breath to steel himself for what needed to be done. "How long till he should be here?"

"He said 45 minutes. I don't know where he was, but it shouldn't be much longer."

Cam'ron sat down on the couch and listened for any approaching vehicles. Within another 15 minutes a car pulled into the driveway with music blasting. Cam'ron peeked out the front window and saw the young dude bopping his head to the beat as he put out a cigarette. He couldn't have been much older than 16 and had no clue that Cam'ron laid in wait on him. He ran up the steps and knocked on the door. Cam'ron moved to the back of the door, so the young dude couldn't see him when Tamara opened the door.

Rita moved quickly into the back room out of sight as Tamara hollered from the couch, "Just a minute!"

When she was certain that everyone was out of sight, she opened the door. The young cat had a smirk on his face when he saw how raggedy Tamara looked. She was wrapped up like a mummy and everyone had heard how she got her ass whipped.

With a smirk on his face he said, "Troy said to take you to the hospital. You ready ta go or what?"

Tamara balled up her face at the dude's attitude, but played her part, "I gotta get my stuff. Come in." As she turned to step away from the door the young cat followed her stepping into the house.

When she was clear of the door Cam'ron raised up and slammed the butt of the gun down on his head. The young dude's head gave off a dense thunk as he tried to run forward to escape the pain. Cam'ron followed him as he ran into Tamara. Tamara yelled and tried to push him away from her and couldn't because of her bruised arms.

Cam'ron reached out and smacked the dude again. He grunted in agony and started flailing blindly as his legs tried to get purchase.

Cam'ron hit him in the side with the butt of the gun after seeing the young dude's head must've been made of steel. The young buck's ribs gave a crunching sound from the impact of the blow and he crumpled balling up into the fetal position. Cam'ron stood over top of him and pointed the gun right into the young buck's open mouth as he gasped for air.

The young buck's eyes went wide as a fish while he cringed with the gun in his mouth.

Cam'ron smiled, "Wanna live motherfucker? Cause I ain't got much time. Now where the fuck is your boss at?"

The young buck looked terrified and nodded that he'd give up the tapes. Cam'ron pulled the gun out of his mouth so he could talk and had to knock him out to shut him up afterwards.

He put the young motherfucker in the trunk of Rita's car and rolled out to meet Smash at June and Drag's drop spot.

****

Smash pulled up to the back woods drop spot. He pulled alongside of the trailer, popped the trunk and stepped out of the car. He grabbed his bag of treats he'd brought especially for Summer, hefted it over his shoulder, then walked to the back of the car.

Summer lay in the fetal position with eyes bulging in horror. Her hair was disheveled and her cat suit was torn in places that showed blood caked wounds.

"Party time bitch!" Smash said as he puffed his signature Dutch with a sick grin on his face. He grabbed Summer by her hair and dragged her out of the trunk. She fell like a caught fish and Smash showed no mercy as he pulled her to her feet and hit her with three body shots.

"Walk ho!"

Summer limped beside him as he held her up by one arm with her hands behind her back. She favored her right leg since portions of her left foot were missing from Cam'ron's well placed shot.

Drag opened the door with cane in hand, "Been spectin you Baby! I see we got a guest too! Cam'ron should be here real soon. Let me see who you brought to the party!"

When Summer stepped into the light of the open door, Drag's eyes squinted in recognition. "I know her. Das one of Mickey's girls!"

Cam'ren was laying on the couch listening to all of this and at the mention of Mickey's name got up off the couch. The name had stuck in his head for all of these years. It had haunted him since the day that he saw his father killed, and now he'd heard it again.

Cam'ren moved up behind Drag and got a good look at Summer.

His whole personality changed. "Bring that bitch up in here! She's the one that killed my father!"

Drag had to push him back before he could get out the door. Smash was caught off guard by hearing that Summer had something to do with killing Cam'ron's father. Now he understood the reaction of the two at the graveyard.

Summer tried to pull away in terror and Smash had to drag her the rest of the way to the steps as she cried and pleaded through the gag in her mouth.

June moved up to help Smash get her into the house as Drag tried to calm Cam'ren down.

"Young Buck! Be cool man. You gon get all

the revenge you need. We got the bitch and we gon handle dis shit. Just be cool!"

Cam'ren calmed himself as they brought Summer into the trailer and sat her in a chair. They tied her down while Smash put down his bag then walked over to Cam'ren.

"Listen my dude, we gonna torture this bitch right, then we gonna get that motherfucker who killed yo peoples, ya heard? Jus be cool. Cam'ron be here soon."

Cam'ren calmed down and looked at Drag. "You know this bitch, and you know who Mickey is?"

Drag let him go since he seemed to be calm enough, "Yeah I know Mickey. I did time in the feds with him. That niggah is a joint! He was fuckin and suckin every homo in the pen. He was gettin money running number houses and gamblin joints back in the day, but I ain't know he was out of the feds! This was one of his girls from back in the day, but I ain't seen "her" in years. I thought she was dead!"

As they talked, another car could be heard coming up the dirt road. Drag went to the door to see who was coming. Cam'ron pulled up and popped his trunk as he got out.

"Damn Baby! You just in time!" Drag answered from the door.

Cam'ron laughed, "I had to pick somethin up on the way!" He said, as he pulled open the trunk and dragged the young punk out of the car and pulled him to his feet.

Drag squinted trying to see who he'd brought with him. "I'ma have to start chargin you motherfuckers admission man. We got us a full fuckin house!"

He stepped to the side to let them both in. The young cat looked terrified, but gave no resistance as Cam'ron escorted him into the trailer and sat his ass on the couch Cam'ren had been laying on.

Cam'ren walked over and hugged his brother. "I handled that with the police bro. Er' thing gon be aiight, ya heard."

Cam'ren nodded as he looked into his twin brother's eyes. He'd been faced with a choice, and chosen his brother for better or for worse.

Now it was time for pay back on all the motherfuckers who'd destroyed him and his brother's life.

If it hadn't been for the bitch that was sitting in the chair in front of them, they would've had a father in their life. If it hadn't been for the motherfucker that she worked for, he wouldn't have had to choose between his adopted father and his brother, and would've had a father to raise them.

Now it was time for the Summer who sat spitting images of their father P-Love, and she understood why they held so much anger for her.

Smash reached into his bag and pulled out a drill. He extracted two long screws out of his pocket and smiled. "I say we light this bitch up! Can't have a party without fireworks my dude."

Cam'ren stepped up, "I'ma handle this shit," and took the drill as his brother watched.

"Get me a car battery and some jumper cables!"

Smash went back out to the car to retrieve what Cam'ren wanted. As he searched for the jumper cables he could hear the drill go off along with the muffled screams of Summer.

When he got back, Cam'ren had his shirt off and was drilling one of the screws into the side of Summer's head.

"Damn my dude, you ain't playin no games!" He said as he stepped back in with the battery and jumper cables. June and Drag sat in the kitchen playing cards, as if nothing so gruesome as torture was taking place in the next room.

Cam'ron held Summer's head still as Cam'ren drilled the other large screw into her skull. Each time she looked as if she was ready to faint, he smacked her back to consciousness.

The young buck on the couch was balled up like a little bitch crying his eyes out in fear.

Smash sat the battery down beside the chair and stepped back to watch the show. Summer began to have a seizure, so they waited for it to pass before continuing. Cam'ron removed the gag while Cam'ren attached the jumper cables to the battery and made them spark by touching them to one another.

"Now bitch, we can make this fast or slow. Either way I'm gon enjoy it. Where the fuck is

Mickey?"

Summer gasped for air and looked around incoherently. When she finally focused, Cam'ron slapped her again, "Where the fuck is Mickey bitch?"

Summer's head lolled for an instant as she moaned, but didn't answer.

Aiight, since you ain't gonna talk, light her ass up!"

Cam'ren touched the negative and positive ends of the jumper cables to the screws in Summer's head as she jerked with every muscle in her body seizing up, Cam'ren touched the screws for only an instant as he didn't want her to die.

They waited a while until Summer regained consciousness. "Now I'ma ask you one more time bitch. I don't think you can take much more of this. Where the fuck is Mickey?"

Summer mumbled incoherently for a second, and Cam'ron had to get up on her to hear, "Clair-- mont, Clair-mont," she whispered almost inaudibly.

"Clairmont Road? Is that where he's at?"

Summer nodded, and Cam'ron briefly remembered a few years back that he'd dropped Troy off at a spot on Clairmont Road. It was starting to come together. He'd claimed he had to see an associate about something and needed a ride since his car was getting fixed. Cam'ron didn't ask any questions and just dropped him off. Now he was starting to wonder whether or not the two of them had been conspiring against him all that time.

He asked Summer, "Who is Mickey to Troy?"

Summer looked up, "Da-da-dad."

Cam'ron and Cam'ren were shocked. Even Smash whistled and stepped in. "I told you that niggah wasn't cool man! He been gunnin for you all along!"

Cam'ron was seeing red. "Kill dis ho!"

Cam'ren touched the two ends of the cables to Summer's head and held them there. She spasmed and wreathed in pain as her hair fell out and her temples turned a soot black color where the screws were in her head. Her eyes sizzled and blood ran from her nose as he continued to let her brain fry.

Smash had to grab him and take the cables off of him as a sick look twisted his face. "Damn my dude! Das enough, the bitch is dead!"

Cam'ron walked over to the couch and pulled the .38 he'd gotten from Rita and Tamara. "How many cat's Troy got watchin his spot wit em?"

The young dude pissed himself as Cam'ron removed his gag, "Jus two! Jus two, I swear!"

Cam'ron nodded, "Well here go two for you pussy," and let off two shots to the young dudes skull.

POP! BOP!

Drag came limping into the living room with a cigarette hanging out of the side of his mouth.

"Y'all motherfuckers done ruined my crib man! It's gonna take us forever ta clean this shit up!"

Cam'ron turned to his Old Head, "Don't worry Old Head, I'ma buy you a new trailer when this shit is over wit."

Drag laughed as June stood behind him smiling, "Man you know I'm jus fuckin wit you. Just get rid of these motherfuckers and handle-yo business, so we can get back to makin dis money, ya heard?"

With that said, Smash, Cam'ron, and Cam'ren started loading the bodies into the car to get rid of them in the back woods. By the time they were done, it was early morning and they were all exhausted.

CHAPTER 20

Pam tossed and turned in her hotel bedroom. Her mother was in the room next door in what she hoped was relative safety from Troy and the people who worked for him.

She rolled over and grabbed her cell phone to check the time. As she yawned and scrolled through her phone to also check her messages from the house, she noticed the number of the clinic where she'd recently had her abortion.

She didn't know why they were calling her and decided to shower before getting back to them on the phone. She showered and got dressed to go and eat breakfast. Right before leaving she popped open her phone and dialed the clinic's number.

"Free Clinic, how may I help you?" The voice answered on the other end.

"Yes, I'm returning a call you placed to me?"

"Name please?" The voice responded.

Pam gave her name and was put on hold to be connected with her doctor.

After a few minutes, the doctor came to the phone. "Pam? I'm calling to give you the results of your tests we ran on you before your abortion. I'm afraid I have some troubling news for you.

Would you like to come in or should I just

give you the results over the phone?"

Pam didn't know what the hell the doctor was talking about.

She'd had STDs before and expected that perhaps Troy had given her something she would have to get a shot for.

"I can't come in right now, I'm out of town. You can give me the results over the phone and I'll get whatever shots I need when I get where I'm going."

The doctor cleared her throat, "Well, I'm sorry to be the one to have to tell you this, but what you have is going to require far more than a shot. You're HIV positive."

Pam nearly fainted in shock. She looked at the phone as if she were lost in the twilight zone, while the phone kept speaking to her.

"Hello? Hello? Pam are you still there?"

Pam dropped the phone and began to weep uncontrollably. She thought of how her life had changed because of her affair with Troy. She wasn't sure of when she contracted the disease, and was grateful of the fact that she hadn't slept with Cam'ron for some time. That at least gave him a chance of not having the disease. Then again, it was also a possibility that Cam'ron could have been the one who gave her the disease as well. She just didn't know.

She tried to gather her senses as she lay crying in the hotel bed for nearly thirty minutes. She tossed over in her mind how she was going to break the news to Cam'ron. Her relationship with him was over either way. If he didn't have it then he'd know that she was cheating on him. That meant death. To know that she was cheating on him with Troy meant an even worse fate, a slow death.

To make matters even worse, if Troy had contracted HIV from her that meant that there was a strong possibility that Smallworld had contracted the virus when he raped her. She'd have to break that news to Rita and Tamara. Smallworld would have to be checked for her own safety.

A plan came to mind in her head. She had to get ghost and she couldn't count on her mother to do what needed to be done.

Her mother wouldn't go for it after all that Cam'ron had done for them.

She gathered herself together and called Tamara's house. Rita answered after the third ring, clearly having just been awakened from her call.

"Hello?"

"Who is this?"

"This is Rita, who is this?"

"Rita, this is Pam. I got some bad news. Is Tamara up?"

"Naw she's sleep. Cam'ron ain't here either. He came past here last night and still has my car. What's up?"

Pam began relaying to Rita the bad news regarding the possibility that Smallworld had HIV. They cried together and talked about how to handle the situation. When they both agreed on how to handle things, they both hung up and started moving.

First Rita called to the hospital to inquire about the welfare of Smallworld's condition. She was stable and resting comfortably. When Rita inquired about her test results, her worst fears were confirmed. Smallworld was also HIV positive and could very well be in the first stage of full blown AIDs.

Rita lost it. She slammed the phone down and ran into Tamara's room.

"Tamara, get up! Get up! You gotta get up!"

Tamara woke drowsily wondering what the heck was wrong with her sister this time.

"What! What Rita! Calm down!" She screamed as her sister kept crying.

When Rita was able to gather herself, she gave Tamara the tragic news. "Troy gave Smallworld HIV and it might be turning into full blown AIDs!"

"Girl you crazy! My daughter ain't got no AIDs. What the hell you talkin about?"

"Troy gave that shit to Pam and she just found out, so I called the hospital to see if her test results came back. They did and confirmed that she got HIV."

Tamara sat stunned. It was too much for her mind to process. She couldn't speak and she couldn't think. The reality that Troy was HIV positive also meant that there was a very good chance that she also had the virus. That her daughter had contracted it was too much for her to fathom.

"Get outta my house! Don't you ever say shit about this to nobody! My baby ain't got no damn AIDs and neither do I! Now get out!"

Rita was shocked. She barely even recognized her sister. She just couldn't accept the reality of what she'd gotten into by dealing with Troy for all those years. She was probably dying along with her daughter, and couldn't deal with it. It was too much for her mind.

Rita got up and went to her room. She couldn't stay if Tamara didn't want her to. She had planned on leaving anyway after talking to Pam. Her sister's response just gave her another excuse.

As she gathered her things, she heard her sister rummaging in her room. Within minutes she heard a shot go off and ran into the room to see what happened. When she was able to get the door opened, her sister lay half in the closet with her brains splattered on the ceiling of the closet. The gun Cam'ron had taken from the young punk lay by her lifeless hand as she twitched momentarily in the last throes of death.

Rita screamed, "Tamara! Nooooo!" As she knelt by her sister weeping uncontrollably. Her mind was overwhelmed with grief and within minutes the shock of everything that happened to her began to turn her heart to stone.

She stood and said her last farewells to Tamara, grabbed her shit, then headed for the door as she called Pam back.

Pam answered on the second ring, "Hello?"

Rita could hear the sadness in her voice. She didn't have anymore sadness to give to the world. She'd had enough.

"We gonna get my niece outta that hospital and we gonna get Cam'ron's money. Then we gonna leave all these motherfuckers behind and live. You hear me girl."

The force and authority that Rita carried in her voice gave Pam strength. She just needed an anchor, and Rita was it.

"How we gon do it?"

Rita began to give her instructions and Pam followed them to the letter.

****

Where da fuck is Tyron at wit da car! He shoulda been back!"

Troy was furious. It was 12:00 the next day and he hadn't heard anything from him or Tamara. He was stuck out in the middle of the woods with no means of moving if he had to with all the coke and money he'd taken from the stash spot.

He didn't know why Smallworld was sick and didn't really give a fuck, so long as the little girl didn't tell on him. He didn't need the aggravation of having to deal with her and her mother's problems right now.

Plus, he hadn't heard anything from

Mickey. He didn't know what the status of the hit was, and not knowing what was going on was starting to take its toll. He ordered his two young guns to spread out and circle the perimeter of the trailer. They were both tired since they hadn't slept since running up on the stash spot. Troy didn't seem to care. His irritation and growing paranoia didn't let him see how he was slippin.

Off in the woods, Cam'ren, Cam'ron, and Smash watched the place in a triangle formation. They communicated from a wireless walkie talkie system they'd bought on the way to where Troy was hiding.

Each carried an AR15 along with the handgun of their choice as a backup.

It took time to move into position because of the heavily wooded area surrounding the trailer. After the woods there was a 50 yard clearing leading up to the trailer.

They saw no cars and very little movement inside of the trailer besides two young men who moved around the perimeter with AK47 assault rifles slung over their shoulders.

If the information that they'd gotten from Tyron before killing him was correct, it was three on three. The problem was that they would easily be seen coming if they tried to approach the trailer outright from any direction. So they had to come up with a plan.

Fortunately, time was on their side since Troy's vehicle disappeared with Tyron.

As Troy lay stewing in his anger, the phone

rang.

"Hello!?" Troy answered anxiously, hoping it was Tyron.

"Troy? This is Pam. I just called to let you know that I know you tried to kill me you punk! You sent that little girl to do what you couldn't do cause you wasn't man enough to do it yourself, "AND" I wanted you to know that you gave me and her HIV! You gonna die a slow death you fuckin bastard!"

Troy was caught completely off guard, "Bitch, I don't know what da fuck you talkin bout! What you mean, HIV?"

"Yo' freak ass gave me HIV and you gave Smallworld HIV too when you raped her! I know what you did, and so does everybody else. You gon die you stinkin bitch!"

Troy was stunned. He didn't know how to respond. Smallworld had exposed him, and to make matters worse, Pam was saying that he'd given both of them HIV. He hung up and began pacing the floor.

Right at that moment, the young dude in the back of the trailer slid off into the woods near where Smash lay hiding to take a piss. It was the opportunity they'd been waiting for.

As the young man leaned his gun up against the tree next to him and undid his pants, Smash rose up into a crouch on the other side of the bushes. He pulled his knife from a sheath tucked in the small of his back and began duck walking to get closer without dude seein him.

When he was in striking distance, he rose up and dove over the heavy brush with outstretched hands slashing furiously for the man's throat.

The young gun barely sidestepped at the last instant causing Smash to miss by mere inches, as the knife flashed where his throat was just milliseconds ago.

Smash rolled forward with his momentum and came up on his feet as he pivoted to face the man before he could grab his rifle.

The young gun's pants being around his waist slowed him as he dove for his gun, causing him to fall clumsily. Smash was on him in seconds stabbing downward with the knife trying to finish the young gun before someone heard the altercation.

The young gun reached and grabbed Smash's wrist trying to impede his knife thrust. It became a battle of strength with Smash on top. He drew back his other hand and bashed the young man across his face while he was defenseless with both hands on his knife arm.

The young gun grunted and tried to bite Smash in a feeble attempt to delay the inevitable. He bit down hard on Smash's knife hand and Smash had to bite back his desire to scream in pain.

He dug into the young gun's right eye socket like it was a bowling ball. The young man screamed out in agony as pain shot through his head. He released his bite on Smash's knife arm in doing so, and loosened his grip as he reached to remove Smash's finger from his eye socket. In that split second Smash followed through with his knife hand and planted the knife into his throat, just as he let out his scream.

With fury he twisted the knife digging deep for the young man's spine with the blade of the knife.

In seconds, the last gurgling breaths of the young gun were spent and Smash was on the move towards the rear of the trailer.

As he moved, he called through his walkie talkie, "I'm clear in the rear. Hit em now!"

Hearing a clear sign, Cam'ron moved up to the edge of the woods and took a shot at the man in the front of the trailer with his AR15.

BOOM! BOOM! BOOM!

He layed down fire, as he tried to find his range on the target.

The young gun in front began running for the cover of the trailer's side while laying down a hail of bullets as he went.

BRRRRIIIP! BIP! BIP! BIP!

He shot blindly as he bent the corner of the trailer, then turned back to see where his target was.

Troy took cover behind furniture inside of the trailer as he moved to see where the shots were coming from. He saw movement to his left from the front window and opened fire with his 357 Magnum.

BLAM! BLAMI BLAM! BLAM!

Cam'ren caught sight of the young gun from

the front moving right around into his line of sight with his back turned. He moved quietly up to the edge of the woods and took aim.

BLAM! BLAM! BLAM!

All three shots hit cleanly and mangled the young man's body as he was thrown into the side of the trailer. Blood, brain matter, and cartilage covered the trailer's side in splatter patterns that belied the bullet's trajectories.

Cam'ren called through his walkie talkie as he moved forward to where the body lay, "I got the one that was in front."

Smash called back, "I'm in the rear, keep him shootin my dude!"

Cam'ron opened fire on the window then hollered out, "Come on out Troy! You baby Rapin snake! I got sum'thin for yo' punk ass!"

Troy fired shots blindly through the window then hollered back, "Come get me you bitch motha fuckah! I got yo' punk right here!"

Cam'ron fired another shot to keep him distracted, then goaded him some more. "I ain't a lil kid niggah! You ain't got nuffin fo' me!"

Troy shot again in response, then paused to reload. As he did, he answered, "That ain't what yo' ho said when I was fuckin her behind yo' back chump!" He began to laugh hysterically. Troy knew it was over. He just wanted to go out with guns blazing.

"Ay Cam'ron, I jus spoke to her too! You know what she told me? She said she got da HIV! So if she got it, dat me you got it too! I got it from fuckin her, so I'ma die anyway, "and" yo' ass gonna go wit us!" He laughed even harder as he continued to load.

He paused as he heard something behind him. He turned trying to aim the gun in the direction of who was behind him. He was too late.

"Lights out my dude!"

Blam! Blam! Blam! Blam! Blam!

Smash fired off all head shots as Troy's head was shattered into tiny pieces from the ferocity of the bullets.

When he was done, he stood over Troy's decimated carcass. "I told yo ass I was gonna get you!"

Cam'ron and Cam'ren moved to the trailer door as Smash gave the all clear sign. Within seconds they were inside and standing over Troy's decapitated body.

They quickly inventoried the contents of the trailer. No one wanted to look at Cam'ron as they all had heard how Pam had betrayed him. That it was possible he had HIV from her cheating ass obviously weighed heavily on him. When all was secured, they both turned to Cam'ron. Cam'ren grabbed his brother before he could leave the trailer.

"Yo' bro! We don't know what that niggah said was true. You gon have to talk to Pam and find out. Don't let that shit get to you. Ya heard?"

Cam'ron shook off his brother's grasp. "We got work to do! We'll deal wit the other shit when thas' done!" Then Cam'ron moved to retrieve his vehicle so that they could start loading up the money and product they'd retrieved.

CHAPTER 21

Cam'ron, Cam'ren, and Smash pulled up to the gates of Mickey's estate on Clairmont. Cam'ron turned to Smash, "Ay yo' dis personal. Meet us back here in 20 minutes."

Smash took a puff of his Dutch, then looked over at Cam'ron and Cam'ren, "Y'all sure y'all don't need no help?"

Cam'ron appreciated the love. Smash was always down as a comrade, it was just that this was family business him and Cam'ren had to settle.

"Naw my dude, we gon handle dis here cause this is family business, ya heard? But I appreciate the love. We'll see you here in twenty."

Smash gave his partner dap, then Cam'ren as they climbed out.

They scaled the brick wall surrounding Mickey's home as he sped off further down Clairmont.

It was nearly 2:00 a.m. in the morning as the twins moved towards the large house.

Every light in the place was out. They wanted to use the element of surprise.

****

Mickey sat in his darkened den with his

homosexual lover.

They were enjoying their last moments of homosexual lust.

They didn't care that they both were about to die since they were dying anyway from the disease.

****

Cam'ron and Cam'ren moved to a back window. Beside it was a wooden trellis within reach of a second floor window.

Cam'ron went first. Finding the window open, he slid in.

Cam'ren followed suit.

They found themselves in a spare bedroom. The hall smelled of shit and Vaseline as they edged their way out of the room. The scent seemed to be wafting from the back stair that faced them, so they moved in that direction as quietly as they could in the dark.

As they crept down the stair, they could hear Tyson grunting like a pig as Mickey rammed himself into Tyson's muscled backside.

Cam'ron edged toward the door that stood ajar at the base of the steps and peeked into the room.

The sight sickened him and as he drew back, he bumped the door.

Cam'ren who stood right behind him moved past him, but by then it was too late.

Mickey and Tyson jumped for their guns

and took cover as Cam'ren burst into the room.

Within seconds Cam'ron recovered and followed looking for a clear shot.

BOP! BOP! BOP! BOP! BOP!

Cam'ren's AR15 sprayed the bookshelves beyond where Mickey and Tyson had just stood.

Mickey peeked from behind his desk and fired low hitting Cam'ren's left knee.

The 45 slug took a chunk of his knee out and caused his aim to stray to the right.

Cam'ron let loose with his AR15 as soon as his brother fell clear.

****

Tyson was slower to react than Mickey and caught a round in the side of his neck.

He screamed like a dog in heat as the blood gushed from a main artery.

He'd be dead in minutes.....

****

Mickey looked at his feet and saw Tyson bleeding out. He slipped from the Vaseline he had on himself. He'd smeared it, as he dove for cover. That slip exposed his upper torso to Cam'ren who lay at Mickey's head level.

He squeezed the trigger.

BOOOOOOOOM!

The AR round ate the top of Mickey's head

off as shrapnel from his skull imbedded itself into the floorboards behind him.

Cam'ron stepped over to where Tyson lay in his last futile gasps for air.

Cam'ron let off another round to Tyson's head that left a shit stain of brain on the carpet.

Cam'ron moved over to help his brother up. When he looked at his knee, he could see that it was bad. His whole knee cap was gone.

He called Smash on his cell as he looked for the front gate mechanism.

"Yo my dude?"

"I need you quick, my brother is hurt! I'm hittin the gate now!"

He hung up and went back to Cam'ren. The bleeding was heavy, so he wrapped his jacket around his leg to staunch the bleeding, then picked him up and carried him to the front door.

Within minutes, Smash was pulling up the long driveway. Together they got him secured in the passenger seat, then took him straight to the hospital.

By the time they arrived, Cam'ren was unconscious from blood loss. They took him into the emergency room. Smash took all of the weapons and left to stash them while Cam'ron waited for a prognosis.

Within hours Smash woas back and sitting in the waiting room to see how Cam'ren was.

It took hours of surgery before they were able to finally get a report.

When the doctor came out to greet them,

they were surprised to see that the doctor recognized Cam'ron as Shirley and P-Love's son. Dr. Sharpe had treated Cam'ron and Cam'ren's mother for cancer all those years ago, and he remembered him.

He approached Cam'ron with so much familiarity that it kind of threw Cam'ron off.

"AHH! You must be Cam'ron. Pleased to meet you young man!"

Cam'ron couldn't tell if it was some kind of sick joke being played on him or not. He shook the man's extended hand cautiously.

Dr. Sharpe could see that Cam'ron didn't recognize him and reminded him of who he was. "I used to work here with your mother and I treated her many years ago. I wanted to come down and let you know personally how your brother is doing."

Cam'ron let out a sigh of relief.

Dr. Sharpe smiled, "Listen, everything is gonna be just fine. Your brother lost a lot of blood and we'll have to rebuild his knee, but I've got the best doctors taking care of him. He should be fine."

Smash and Cam'ron were elated at the news.

The Doctor could see that he'd eased their minds. Then he gave them the bad news. "The only problem you'll have is that he'll need some months of therapy. We're gonna have to rebuild everything. But as I said, he'll be able to walk again."

Cam'ron and Smash didn't care. As far as they were concerned, he wasn't playing professional sports, so it really didn't matter. Cam'ren would live. That's all they cared about.

The doctor shook their hands and advised them to come back the next day. That would give Cam'ren enough time to recover from the surgery.

The next day, Cam'ren was up and watching the news.

Cam'ron and Smash came in to see him. All of them were happy to be alive.

They'd weathered the betrayal of everyone else around them and survived through loyalty to one another.

In the end, it was their Bullet Proof Love for each other that had gotten them through everything that they'd faced in the last two weeks.

They had avenged P-Love's death. Now the big choices about how to rebuild things lay in front of them.

Cam'ren didn't know yet whether he was going to be accepted into the feds, and even if he did, he couldn't pass the physical.

In all honesty, he didn't even care about becoming a cop anymore, let alone becoming a lawyer. He wanted in on the family business and a chance to move like Gangsters Moved.

It was in his bloodline, and it showed at crunch time.

They hugged each other cheerfully.

"Glad to see you made it!" Cam'ron said as he leaned over and gave his brother a hug.

"Glad to see you too Cam'ron.

Smash followed suit like one of the family, "Yo my dude! I guess you ain't gonna be racin after dem hoes no time soon, huh?" He joked as he gave Cam'ren a hug.

"They got enough pretty nurses here. Trust me. I think that's why Daddy worked here for so long!" Cam'ren shot back, as he smiled at his twin brother.

As they exchanged pleasantries, Dr. Sharpe walked in with Cam'ren's chart.

"Ah good! You're all here so I can give you the news. Your surgery turned out splendidly! We had to replace your knee, but you'll be up and moving around in a few weeks."

As he said this, news that Mickey's body had been found in the house flashed across the screen. Dr. Sharpe and the three men listened intently. When the broadcast was done, Dr. Sharpe looked to Cam'ren and Cam'ron.

Dr. Sharpe smiled at both of the men. "The funny thing is we never did find a bullet. It must've gone clean through." He said, then he winked at the three men.

All three of them gave a sigh of relief. If the bullet that took out Cam'ren's knee would've been linked to Mickey's death, Cam'ren would've certainly gone to jail.

The doctor continued, "You know I always liked your mother and your father. They were both good people. You boys stay out of trouble and give me a call if you ever need anything."

Cam'ron stopped the doctor before he was about to leave, "Actually doc, there is one thing you could do for all of us."

The doctor looked puzzled, "And what might that be?"

"Give us a test for AIDS and HIV," they all answered in unison.

The doctor smiled and shook his head as he called for a nurse to instruct her to draw their blood for the tests, then walked away with one last goodbye.

****

Within days, Cam'ron began to pick up the pieces of his business.

When he was finally able to return to his home, Pam was gone along with $2.5 million dollars of his money.

He'd gotten the results back from his test. He didn't have anything show up on his bloodwork.

He redistributed the remaining coke he'd taken back from Troy through Drag and June. He had a lot of catching up to do to secure his place in the streets again.

Within weeks, Troy and Summer's bodies were found dead and stinking in the Santee River along with Tyron's body.

Sunshine's death was considered a botched

robbery, while Mickey's death remained unsolved.

Within weeks after having discovered that he'd passed the bar, Cam'ren received a letter at his home beside his brother's estate. It had a return address from the Federal Bureau of Investigation.

Cam'ren opened it as his brother sat with him inside of his new private office, waiting to hear the news.

Cam'ren opened the envelope and when he was done reading, he looked up.

"They accepted me bro! Upon completion of a physical, I'm to begin training to be a fed!"

Cam'ron smiled, and so did Cam'ren as they both looked at his cane.

With a glint in his eye, Cam'ron leaned forward toward where his brother sat resting his leg on a divan.

"Looks like we gon' have ta switch."

Then they both laughed, as they put together their next moves....

EPILOGUE

Tank lay sleeping in his palatial mansion in Miami Florida as a cool breeze wafted into his room off the ocean.

With the ruffle of his linen curtains moved a shadowy figure.

It moved quietly on padded shoes in all black.

A glint from the nine millimeter's silencer flashed momentarily in the mirror as he rose up beside Tank's bed.

The two women that lay entangled with him in his sheets never heard the killer as he approached.

Tank turned to fondle ass cheeks, he looked up to see the dark figure standing over him with the long nozzle of the silencer pointed directly at his forehead.

The red dot lighting up his forehead marked the trajectory of the assassin's bullet as the voice whispered its greetings.

A gift from the Shabazz Brothers.

VIP! VIP! VIP!

All three of the bed's occupants lay dead with holes in their craniums.

Cameron's connect for distribution of cocaine throughout the entire South was dead on the explicit orders of Hassan Shabazz.

The first moves of a takeover in the South had begun.

Cameron's connect was only the first casualty......

****

Pam and Rita had taken up residence in Miami.

They'd buried Smallworld who died giving birth to Troy's child, then settled into the routine of caring for her child as a family.

They never looked back on the life they left behind. They tried to build a new life for as long as they could have it.

With the money that they'd taken from Cam'ron, they were able to get Pam the best medicine that money could buy.

She was happy for the time that she had with Rita and Smallworld's child. Their love gave her comfort as she battled with her disease.

What neither of them knew was that fate would not let them live in peace for long.

More chaos was coming, and their paths would eventually lead them back to the man that they'd betrayed.......

Read gangster Moves Part 2 (The Switch) to see what happens next!!!!!

ABOUT THE AUTHOR

Yusuf Ali Mitchell was born in the South Philly section, on 7th Street. His mother bought a house down in 5th Street Projects, and they moved down there in the 80's going back and forth until Yusuf moved back down there.

He loves the outdoors, fishing and all those types of things. He loves being around his family and children and grew up in the Nation of Islam, until he converted over to Sunni Islam.

He has been locked up in SCI Dallas for six years where he achieved his GED, and met a few good friends, that today he can call his brothers.

What inspired Yusuf to write was reading his first book by Sidney Sheldon, and Donald Goines. These are the writers that he looked up too.

When he first came to jail in the late 90's he was at a third grade reading level because Yusuf chose the streets over school. He went, but he wasn't there mentally. Jail made him a man, and taught him everything he needed.

Today Yusuf is at a college level, and plans to go much further, looking forward to making movies, and setting up nonprofit organizations for Lupus, and Cancer, and Sickle Cell.

Yusuf's message to everyone is whatever

you put your mind to, you can achieve it. Jus
keep at it and don't stop. Many have told him tha
he wouldn't make it to be 18.

His body has been locked up, but his min
is elsewhere. Always know, if people are talkin
about you, then you're doing something right.

Thank
You

Follow The Hood Novelist on Social Media, for upcoming book signings and to stay in the loop for upcoming book releases.